Benjamin
By Robert Scheige

Copyright © 2014 Robert Scheige.

All rights reserved. No part of this publication may be reproduced, distributed, or transmitted in any form or by any means, including but not limited to mechanical or electronic methods, without the express written consent of the author.

ISBN-13:   978-1503356658
ISBN-10:   1503356655
BISAC: Fiction / Literary Fiction

This is a work of fiction, except for "Bounties", which is sadly true.

Book design by Robert Scheige.

Cover illustration by Brian Garabrant.
www.briangarabrant.com

This is dedicated to Benjamin, who didn't deserve to die alone.

Contents

I.	On the Ice	1
II.	The Rising Son	39
interlude	Van Diemen's Land	87
III.	The Chamber	95
epilogue	The Earth Itself Breaking	163

Preface

I don't really know what got into me, but one night a seed of an idea popped into my head and the next thing I knew I was writing a book.

"Benjamin" began as a standalone short story about a hunter and was only later expanded into the three interlocking stories found in this volume. After I finished writing the hunter's story, which was more or less in the same form found here, I moved on to the next project and started writing an altogether separate novel. Still something kept calling me back to the anguished world of the hunter, perhaps because I found it so eerily similar to our own. It seemed as if there was more that needed to be shown, more angles to explore, more story to tell.

Then one day it came to me, almost all at once, ideas for Acts II and III, so I shelved the other novel I had been developing and switched gears. Many a night was spent outlining and then drafting these new Acts, and after reading the initial drafts I immediately saw the thematic connections and ways in which the three stories, which themselves are relatively straightforward and self-contained, evoke new meanings and offer a more complete picture if read as a single work. As I continued drafting, editing, rearranging, and refining Benjamin, the whole picture slowly came into view and I was able to more fully realize my vision.

Writing this book was a balancing act. On one end I wanted to produce an art piece, something that could be understood on several levels, a book complex enough that it could be read and appreciated multiple times. On the other end I wanted to write an engrossing story that would keep readers engaged, wondering what happens next, surprised and satisfied with what they find. Sometimes these two goals were at odds with one another, and I'd have to figure out how to make things work without compromising the broader design.

The key to understanding Benjamin is to recognize that it, in its heart, is a surrealist piece—at least in my opinion. Its contents are meant to appear as a Möbius strip where many aspects of the stories interact and fold back on themselves, both symbolically and thematically. A careful reader may note that unrelated characters share common descriptive traits and that critical events are retold from a different point-of-view or in a familiar, yet altered way. These are intentional and are meant to enrich the story and offer clues to possible explanations. In the end, I have my own interpretation of Benjamin, but it is meant to be open to any reader.

Writing Benjamin was—at different times—exciting,

Benjamin

frustrating, entertaining, and heartbreaking. But overall, it was enjoyable, and something that I've been working on with an almost compulsive bent for the better part of a year.

I hope you find as much enjoyment reading it as I've had writing it. Thank you for taking the time to read my work.

Robert Scheige
February 2015

Benjamin

"When thou tillest the ground, it shall not henceforth yield unto thee her strength; a vagrant and wanderer shalt thou be on the earth."

-Genesis 4:12

I. On the Ice

"There is no witness so dreadful, no accuser so terrible, as the conscience that dwells in the heart of every man."

-Polybius

1
The Deer

Of the exact time and location, he was unsure. But it was cold, getting colder, and as the sun began its inevitable descent towards the horizon he feared the dark that soon would come.

A few inches of snow had fallen and the breeze produced powdery drifts against the winter-dead trees. The sylvan expanse was riddled with melancholy brown tree trunks and twisted branches, as far as he could see, which was in these woods not far at all. For hours he had trudged through the forest, his frustration swelling with each step while his rifle weighed against his shoulder and his prey remained unfound.

Insulated boots and thick socks were essential in these conditions, yet no panacea against the unrelenting cold. His feet felt like blocks from the protracted hike, his toes numb, his legs biting against the crescendo wind, his hands raw in a visceral protest against gloves which were, perhaps for the first time, insufficient.

Inclined to capitulate and return to his cabin, prepared to accept the failure of his pursuit of the unseen, the hunter paused when a deerlike silhouette emerged in the distance. Like a phantom in the wind, it materialized slowly out of the white desolation before vanishing again into the void.

Where the silhouette had appeared, cloven footprints lay neatly on the ground. Where they began was unclear, but they continued forward, deeper into the woods and deeper into the lashing wind which now screamed into the hunter's face like a tempest. He nestled his head deep into his frost rimmed hood as he forged ahead, but even this provided little relief. With his chin down to focus on the tracks rapidly disappearing in the wind, the hunter followed.

He descended into a clearing where he was mystified at the sudden cessation of wind. At the bottom of a hill was a lake of ice whose entire expanse remained unseen to him due to its wandering shoreline and jutting outcroppings. The hunter followed the cloven tracks down to the edge of the lake where they abruptly ended—the deer had walked out onto the ice.

In the absence of tracks, finding the deer meant locating where it had exited the ice. By following the shore he expected, in time, to find hoof prints leading off the ice and to his victim. And so the hunter walked along the bank, untold paces suffering the cold burn of the air, until once more he found the tracks—only these were the same ones he had followed to the lake.

He had come full circle.

If the deer had walked onto the ice, but never off the ice, it had to still be on the ice. Yet he had detected no deer despite being able to see clear across from every point around the lake's rambling waterline. There didn't seem to be any way he could have missed it since he had paid such close attention to his surroundings the entire time. So if the deer was not *on* the ice—could it have fallen *through* the ice?

The hunter again considered returning to his cabin, for the sun had now descended below the horizon, heralding an imminent darkness. The nights here were colder even than the days, and journeying to his cabin in the pitch black was a terrifying proposition for a man alone. Nevertheless, ignoring his own peril he walked onto the ice to find where the deer had fallen through. He could not leave the riddle unsolved.

The ice by the shore was solid for many paces and the hunter had to plant each foot straight down to avoid sliding. Time and again he faltered but never did he fall. When the ice darkened he could tell there was liquid water beneath him. As he continued towards the center of the lake, the ice became thinner with every footfall. Once silent by the shore, his steps started to creak and then to groan. He began to crawl to disperse his weight and the ice bestowed its frigid punishment against his knees. Then, as the ice groaned louder with each quadrupedal motion, he lay on his belly and slid.

At the lake's center the hunter cautiously rose to survey the surface. He saw neither deer nor any holes in the continuous, undisturbed white sheet. If the deer had fallen through, no evidence remained. It was lost, and for a moment the hunter feared he too might suffer a mysterious evanescence, but then with trepidation at each step, he returned to *terra firma*.

Darkness had fallen and the sky had become overcast. The temperature continued its stubborn march downwards. Armed with only a flashlight against the inky blackness, the hunter negotiated the forest and began the long road home.

2
Crossing Paths

Sharp crunches were the consequences of every step, their sounds magnified in the windless silence, as the hunter advanced through the forest. The incandescent spray of his flashlight deflected off the snow, filling the woods with its pale expression.

Nary a star flickered in the overcast sky, and when, for a moment, the hunter turned off his flashlight the blackness surrounding him was absolute. He thought perhaps he could hear his own heart beating. He dreaded what revelation might await him in the darkness, but when he turned his flashlight back on, he was still alone. With feet throbbing at the ache of each frozen step, he continued.

Deep in the forest, he stumbled upon the impressions of a man. These footprints were fresh, appeared to be of someone in flight, and were perpendicular to his path. There shouldn't be anyone else in these woods, the hunter thought, and as he studied the footprints receding towards the black horizon, he wondered with whom he shared these woods. He crossed the man's path and continued.

At last he approached his cabin, a single room outpost in the wilderness, a presence evidenced by the hum of a generator. There was only one road in, unpaved, twisting through the woodland for miles until dead ending at the cabin. The cabin had been in his family long enough that its memory was lost in time, and the hunter somehow felt part of him had always been there.

As he entered the cabin his flashlight sputtered and died, so with his hands up he shuffled through the jet blackness, stumbling through the musty interior, seeking the frayed string hanging beneath a bulb, wondering if perhaps a cervine apparition awaited him in the darkness.

The hunter eventually abandoned his search for the string and located the refrigerator by its sound. The irony of having a refrigerator in this tundra-like weather was not lost on him, but it kept some of his perishables above freezing.

The hunter opened the refrigerator door and admired the chunks of venison from a recent kill, much of it in the refrigerator since the freezer side had overflowed. In this weather he could have left the meat almost anywhere, but the refrigerator at least kept it contained where wildlife might not so easily detect it. With the refrigerator door ajar to allow some light into the room, he found the string and pulled. Released at last from the darkness, he exhaled when the cabin's brown and burgundy wood were revealed.

The hunter grabbed a few logs from the porch and built a fire. He changed out of his snow pants and greatcoat and sat by the fireplace in thermals and heavyweight socks. He had hoped to swiftly warm his frozen body, but his frustration mounted as he continued shivering, cradling his knees against his chest long after the flames had been kindled. While his extremities and front would eventually thaw, the frigid sting behind him continued, and the cold air pressing down on the back of his neck and ears never abated.

Once settled, the hunter grabbed a bottle of whiskey. The bite of the spirit, the tingling on his lips and under his tongue were refreshing, but he preferred his whiskey on the rocks.

He went out to the porch where he kept a cooler of ice. The temperature had been below zero all day yet the cooler was somehow full of water. He stared at it, mouth slightly agape, but eventually shrugged and left it open—yet another strange occurrence in a day full of strangeness. By daybreak surely the cold would prevail and it will be filled with a block of ice, so he thought. He tore an icicle down off the gutter, broke it into several pieces, and dropped them into a glass of whiskey.

3
Imprisoned

In the mind of the hunter lingered the vanished deer—he could think of nothing but. How could it have gone onto the ice, never to return? It might as well have walked out into the ocean.

In theory the deer could have fallen through the ice, especially where it was delicate towards the lake's center, but in the absence of supporting evidence this seemed impossible. Surely he would have noticed a hole large enough for a deer, and yet he had seen no hole at all. So where did it go? Had he missed the exit tracks when circumnavigating the lake?

There was only one way to know for sure—return to the lake and reconnoiter the shoreline. The night had been placid and windless so the tracks should still be there. They *must* still be there.

He left the cabin and began the long pilgrimage to the lake. The weather again was cold, well below freezing but not as stark as the day before. The hunter dressed a little more warmly, perhaps overcompensating, and felt a light layer of sweat on his lower back.

Benjamin

After miles of hiking through the forest, the hunter once again reached the lake. The hoof prints seemed undisturbed overnight, almost as if fossilized in the chalky snow. They terminated at the water's edge as though the deer had evaporated into some sort of wintery netherworld. The hunter again walked along the meandering bank, stepping over rocks and frozen, snow covered sludge. After rounding a bend where a cliff jutted into the lake, the hunter once again descended to the icy shore.

And there, at last, he found his quarry.

A trembling doe was a few paces off the shore, alive but immobile on the ice. Its front legs were bent at the knee and icebound above its hooves. Its back legs were spread eagle behind it and its belly was stuck to the white sheet much like a tongue would be if one were foolish enough to lick a metal pole in the dead of winter. Upon sight of the hunter it tried to rise but was completely anchored by the frozen surface.

The hunter approached the doe but the closer he went the more panicked it became. It flailed and contorted its body in all directions, struggling to rise from the ice, its back hooves finding no purchase, its front hooves unable to move at all. Where its belly was stuck to the ice, fur tore off the skin with each thrashing. The doe snorted and wheezed in distress and in pain and the hunter paused, fearing its flight attempts would result in broken legs or worse.

This was a sad sight indeed. A harrowing sight. The hunter had seen deer shot, hit by cars, even their carcasses ravaged by wolves—but this was different. This animal was utterly helpless on the ice. Its futile escape attempts had turned into acceptance and surrender as it lay there like a blinking cadaver.

How could he have missed this the day before, when he had followed the entire shoreline? The deer was only paces away, how could he have walked right by it? Could he have been so focused on finding the exit tracks that he had completely missed the obvious? And what about when he had been on the ice, at the very center of the lake? He had looked in all directions; surely he would have noticed the deer!

Despite these questions, the hunter quickly stopped thinking about the past and focused on what to do next. Would he complete this hunt and shoot the deer? He had, after all, spent hours tracking the animal and had paid his dues—he had earned his game. Yet here it was, hopeless on the ice, degraded and imprisoned in a humiliating position. The doe stared at the hunter with mournful brown eyes and waited.

The hunter grimaced with indecision despite raising his rifle and pointing it between the eyes of the deer. He would shoot it with a decisive blast to put it out of its misery and be done with it. At this range he would blow its head clean off—this animal's bust would never be a trophy on his wall. Time stood still as the hunter and doe stared at one another—the hunter through the sights of his rifle, the doe from its icy prison below—two partners to a silent dance, both perhaps seeking a distant sympathy.

Had the deer resigned itself to fate or had it no

comprehension of its impending doom? A light breeze began to blow and the hunter's arm became heavy. He lowered the rifle—he could not murder this defenseless creature.

With the mystery of the deer solved, the hunter turned and began the long walk home. As he retraced his steps along the shore, he thought perhaps he heard a whimper from afar, but never looked back.

4
The Pet Store

Back at the cabin, the hunter grabbed a chunk of venison from the fridge and cooked it into a bloody medium rare char. He chewed the meat beside the fire and wiped a trickle of blood from his chin while staring into the flames. He swallowed the last bite and poured himself a glass of whiskey.

He looked at the bottle, half empty with its sullied brown spirit, its frosted surface stinging his fingers and palm.

The hunter went out to the porch and found to his surprise that the cooler was not filled with the block of ice he had anticipated the night before, but with a slushy incertitude that was again deficient for his purposes. He shattered another icicle and quaffed the whiskey.

The deer.

The deer.

He could not erase from his mind that pitiful creature stuck on the ice.

Why didn't he shoot it and put an end to its misery? The animal had been in his sights yet somehow he had been absent the will to finish the deed. For days he had hunted a deer, any deer, feet aching with each step, face frozen from the wind, hands numb from the suffocating cold. Finally he had found it—but could not pull the trigger.

He poured another glass of whiskey.

The hunter remembered when, as a child, he had captured a garter snake in the woods behind his home. He had kept it in a small tank where it was mostly dormant, spending its days coiled behind a rock in the corner. He had fed it crickets and other insects that he would catch behind the shed out back much like he had caught the snake. The snake only fed every ten days or so, and sometimes the crickets would share the tank with it and die long before they became a meal. The crickets never seemed fearful; they were either unaware of the threat lurking beside them or perhaps they simply accepted their fates.

The hunter poured another glass of whiskey.

One day the snake was gone. The tank was closed, so at first his parents assumed that he had set it free; there was no other explanation for its disappearance. Meanwhile, he had blamed his parents, saying it was they who had released the animal. The three searched the house, trying to figure out where the snake had gone and how it had escaped. He mimicked their anxiety so his parents would not seriously suspect an inside job. After scouring the house for hours they gave up, realizing the snake was truly gone, and the hunter feigned devastation at the loss of his friend.

His parents had offered to buy another snake to assuage him, so they went to the local pet store where a baby boa constrictor happened to be for sale. The hunter had been absorbed with this creature, but his parents cautioned that this was no garter snake—the boa could one day be ten feet long and weigh fifty pounds. Nonetheless, he persisted, and his parents soon relented.

At the pet store, he had also seen a tank full of crickets, but the salesman warned that these were not adequate for the diet of such a beast. The salesman took him to the back of the store where a tank teeming with white mice was hidden. There must have been hundreds, maybe even a thousand mice inside, several layers of bodies, some alive, some dead, some perhaps asleep. The living crawled over the dead, the alive over the inert, a mass moving both in chaos and in unison like a fuzzy, filthy white colony. The mice along the perimeter crawled against the glass, some clawing frantically into the clear walls of the fold, desperate to escape their vermin brethren, while others, motionless, stared into nothingness like catatonic prisoners.

The hunter poured another glass of whiskey.

He recalled the way the salesman had pulled out a single, squirming mouse by a pink tail as long as its body. *This* is what you feed a boa, he said, as he dangled the frightened rodent over the snake's tank. He opened his hand as if in absolution, dropping the mouse several feet where it landed with a thud. There was no reason to treat it so inhumanely, the hunter had thought, even if it were to soon become a meal.

Benjamin

Hearing the impact, the boa awoke with a start. It saw the mouse and raised its head well above its curled body. Bruised from its fall and with nowhere to flee, the mouse froze in a trembling panic as it watched the forked ebony tongue of the serpent slither in and out of its mouth. In a blink the boa was across the cage and had the mouse in its deadly embrace, squeezing harder and harder, the mouse flailing and contorting its body in despair until it had been both mentally and physically broken. The boa opened wide and put the whole head of the mouse in its maw. The rodent's tail continued to flop pitifully for several minutes as the snake slowly slid its victim deeper and deeper into its gullet, eating it alive.

You'll have to come back down to the store every couple weeks or so for more food, said the salesman, unless you got mice in your own house, boy. So he did—he returned every two weeks to buy mice, each time watching in horror as the snake consumed yet another quivering mouse. Soon though the endless cycle of sacrifice became too much, and he one day decided to let the boa free to take its chances in the wild, much as he had the garter snake once before.

The hunter looked down at his glass and saw the icicles had melted. Rather than grab another, he put the bottle to his lips and gulped what remained.

Why had he been unable to shoot the deer? Perhaps because it was imprisoned before its predator, much like the mice had been with the boa—without a chance to fight or flee. He had freed the boa as a child to save the mice—or at least to save himself from witnessing their gruesome consumption. Likewise he could try to free the deer, but at what cost? Would he have to tear the skin off its belly and break its legs?

No—freeing the deer seemed unrealistic. It was doomed to remain on the ice, and the hunter always had had difficulty seeing the slow, torturous deaths of innocent creatures. He now had an opportunity to save the deer from its own drawn-out demise by going to the lake at first light to shoot it.

But why wait? I'll do it now, he thought.

As the hunter rose he realized he was on shaky legs. His balance was off and the room was spinning. Perhaps I shouldn't have drunk all that whiskey, he thought, especially with so little food in my belly. The hunter put on his greatcoat, gloves and boots. He grabbed his rifle, put new batteries in his flashlight, and exited the cabin.

By the time he walked out to the porch it had gotten colder, the black night piling its windblown snow against the sides of the cabin. I will not be deterred, the hunter thought, I am going to finish this tonight.

He took two steps down off the porch, slipped on the ice, and plummeted backwards. The last things he remembered while falling were his flashlight hitting him on the side of the head and the sound of footsteps in the distance.

5
Penance

The hunter awoke well before dawn. The back of his head, hair wet with melted ice, lay on the bottom step. Frost was caked on his nose and his head throbbed like the pulse of a bass drum. His rifle and flashlight rested beside him.

The hunter lay there for what felt like forever, his nausea and pounding head so severe that standing simply wasn't an option. But he felt the cold in his bones, its dark suffocation beating down on his body, and knew he must return to the cabin or else he soon may never rise at all.

Only a few withering cinders remained in the fireplace, so the hunter threw in a couple more logs to get the flames going. With each motion the hammering in his head intensified, abusing his whole body with its torment. The hunter took some painkillers, washed them down with ice water from the cooler, and slept by the fire.

6
No One Else but You

It was already midday when the hunter awoke, the fire long gone. His head felt like a swollen fog from his overnight whiskey binge and concussion. Although the pain was far improved from the madness in the night, his vision was blurred, and the hunter wondered just how hard he had hit his head.

Despite the pain and disorientation, the deer continued to dominate the hunter's every reflection. Perhaps he could find some way to allay its woe. He looked around to see what, if anything, there was to bring the deer for sustenance, but he had no food aside from the venison. While he knew that deer could, in desperate times, eat meat, this was too demented for him to consider seriously. There was, however, a general store about twenty miles away and he could probably get there before closing. Surely they will have something to feed the trapped doe, the hunter thought.

He climbed into his truck and drove down the dirt road that snaked through the forest. He must have passed ten miles of monotonous winter wasteland before at last

Benjamin

reaching a paved road. The landscape was overrun with dead trees whose gnarled branches stretched outwards like dirty skeletal fingers, and he wondered if, for them, spring might never come.

Parked in front of the store was a snow-covered pickup, clearly not driven since at least the last snowfall. As the hunter approached the store, he noted the air of abandonment emanating through the cloudy windows in spite of the obfuscated "*Open*" sign blinking in the entryway. A cracked sign over the front door said, quite generically, "*Store*", with the "*e*" hanging as it swayed in the breeze.

A cowbell clanged to announce the hunter's arrival. The air was thick and the store must not have been dusted in years. Some non-perishable foods, sodas, cigarettes, knives, and lighters were for sale but mostly on display were hunting and fishing gear. In the corner he noticed a mousetrap with a moribund rat tangled inside it. As the hunter peered at the gasping, back-broken rodent, the whiskered storekeeper slowly emerged from the back room.

"Damn pests," grumbled the old man. "I'd kill 'em all if I could."

The hunter shrugged. "You just gonna leave it there or are you gonna to kill it?"

"I'll deal with it when I'm good and ready. Listen, if you came down here for more beans and bread, you better have money this time. I ain't trading for firewood no more."

"I think you're confusing me with someone else."

"Am I now?" he snickered. "Ok well what do you want this time?"

"I'm looking for something to feed a doe."

"Don't suggest you do that, baiting is illegal in these here parts."

"I'm not baiting, just feeding."

"Don't you worry about them deer. They'll feed just fine on their own. Been doing it long before you or I were here."

"Not this one."

"If it's old, son, let nature take its course. If it can't make it through the winter on its own then wolves'll find it. They need to eat too, you know."

"She's not old. Just tell me what I can feed her."

"Boy, you shoot it in the leg or something and getting a conscience about it? Just shoot the damn deer in the head and be done with it. It ain't gonna get no better just by feeding it."

"I didn't shoot her in the leg."

"Yeah okay, well you don't need to be feeding no deer. Some of 'em gotta die. That's just the way it is. Woods ain't big enough for 'em all anyway—not anymore."

The two men stared at one another, both entrenched in their positions. The hunter allowed his eyes to wander back towards the mangled rat—its pink tail swatting, its torso twitching, its front paws straining towards him, almost as if begging for help.

"Just show me what I can feed her," said the hunter, returning his gaze to the storekeeper.

Benjamin

The storekeeper narrowed his eyes and shook his head. "Who are you to play god?"

The hunter didn't answer—he just stared, stone-faced, at the old man.

The storekeeper rolled his eyes. "Look, we don't have no fresh fruit this time of year, or any time of year for that matter. Not out here. But there's some canned ones down to your right that maybe you can feed it."

The hunter bought a couple cans of preserved peaches and thanked the storekeeper. As he walked out the door, he recalled the human footprints he had discovered the night before last. "By the way, do you know of anyone else who might be up in these woods?"

"Ain't never been no one else but you up in these woods."

The hunter pondered this for a moment, nodded, and began the long drive back to his cabin.

On the way back, a man on the radio told a story about some teenagers who were arrested after tossing a puppy out of a moving car window. The puppy had been recovered barely alive and was being nourished back to health by veterinarians. While it lost a leg, an eye, and had numerous scars from cigarette burns, the man on the radio told it as an uplifting story because, after all, the dog lived.

7
Warm Impressions

The snow in front of the cabin was covered in dried blood, as if a hundred small feet had stepped in a maroon bath and then traipsed around in white powder. The hunter put the butt of his rifle against his shoulder and pointed the barrel forward before slowly going up the steps. The cabin door was ajar, and when he opened it with the tip of his gun, he was repulsed by the sour smell of urine. The cabin was empty but someone—or some*thing*—had been there. The refrigerator had been overturned and the gore and grease of raw meat was slathered across the dark wood floor.

The hunter went outside and realized the mess out front was actually wolf tracks leading to, and then from, the cabin—an ominous sign since they were headed towards the lake. The hunter followed the paw prints into the woods, expecting a fresh bloodbath at the end of the trail. It was getting colder and little time remained before nightfall.

The wolf tracks ended at the shore, right before the deer, which was improbably alive although unwell. Large impressions in the snow suggested that the wolves had sat there admiring their impending feast for quite some time. However, perhaps engorged from plundering the cabin, they had otherwise ignored the deer and left the area—although no evidence of their departure remained. Maybe they too ventured out onto the ice.

While relieved to find the deer alive, the hunter was dispirited to find it much more worn. Its brown fur seemed dirtier, nappier than before, its eyes drifting between various states of closure. Seeing that the fur and skin of its belly was even more torn, the hunter imagined its frenzy upon sight of the wolves.

The hunter sat down on the wolves' impressions and thought for a moment they might still be warm.

While yesterday the deer flailed and thrashed at the hunter's advance, today it merely stared. It had truly accepted its fate and perhaps even sought a quick end to its frigid imprisonment.

The hunter took off his gloves and opened a can of peaches. The penetrating liquid dripped through his fingertips as he reached forward and fed the deer. The deer consumed the fruit as if it hadn't eaten in weeks.

Once the cans were empty, the hunter returned to the shore and again contemplated bringing the deer swift completion. But again, after raising his rifle and aiming between its eyes, he could not bring himself to pull the trigger.

Oh hell, thought the hunter, maybe I can set it free. I doubt it but maybe.

The deer flinched when the hunter positioned

himself beside it, so he put his palm on its shoulder to communicate that he was here as a friend.

With no large tools but a flashlight and rifle, the hunter lacked the equipment necessary to break the doe free—yet he had to try. The flashlight was far lighter than the rifle, so the weapon would have to do. The hunter raised it with both hands along the barrel, its cold metal stinging through his gloves, and slammed the butt into the ice beside the deer.

At this sudden display of violence, the doe began to thrash and snort hysterically. Its fur began to rip off its belly and the ice shrieked in response to each flailing. The hunter backed off, realizing that this would not do. If he were to free the deer now it would end up mortally injured by its liberation. Perhaps there was another way—he had an icepick back at the cabin, which might allow him to more delicately and quietly free the deer.

Night was coming. He didn't want to journey back to the cabin in the pitch black again, especially not with a pack of wolves prowling about, so he nodded to the deer and commenced the long walk.

"I'll see you soon," said the hunter, while turning.

8
Benjamin

The hunter dreams of a vanishing.

As a dying sun descends below the horizon, shadows of the bars through which the hunter peers glide over the stripes of the prisoner.

The prisoner paces back and forth and back and forth and back and forth and back and forth and back and forth and back and forth and back and forth and back and forth and back and forth and back and forth (until the world goes black forever).

The prisoner is forsaken and hungry. The prisoner is cold.

The prisoner will soon perish. Alone.

The hunter doesn't sleep much that night, but in those few, fleeting moments of introspection, he dreams about Benjamin—locked out of his warm sleeping quarters, curled on a punishing cold cement floor, his last breath a pathetic, whimpering lament of surrender and finality.

9
The Stand

*S*omething large and determined is outside my cabin door, thought the hunter, as he awoke with a start in the dead of the night. But what, or who, could it be? His first instinct was that it must be the deer, deceased and returning to enact vengeance on the man who had chased it to an icy fate before abandoning it to die alone in the cold. But the hunter soon came to his senses since the trespasser sounded heavy and seemed to lumber with a lack of elegance unfit for a deer.

The hunter sat up and grabbed his rifle from beside the bed as the intruder shuffled its heft along the porch. Whoever was out there was looking for a way in. The hunter remained still, sitting upright in his bed, the cabin tranquil and black save the few remaining embers crackling in the fireplace.

Outside, however, was a different environment as the windows were beaten by squalls that seemed to never ebb. Perhaps there was no one out there at all, thought the hunter—it was simply the wind playing tricks on him.

The hunter rose from bed and listened carefully,

trying to determine where exactly the intruder was. The scraping seemed to have stopped so whoever was out there may have departed. When he opened the door the cutting air exploded into the cabin. He peeked out, his rifle cocked and ready to blast any threat lurking in the darkness.

To the left—nothing.

To the right—nothing.

Both directions veiled in a mist of windblown snow.

He crept down the porch and into the pother, his rifle aimed forward and set. With the wind in his face he grimaced and squinted while pushing forward, his breath trailing behind him.

Once he had inspected the porch and found nothing, the hunter decided that it must have indeed been the wind. As he lowered his rifle, an enormous brown paw suddenly came from behind and slapped the side of his head, forcing him to the ground. Landing on his belly, he dropped the rifle which, after several clumsy plunks, bounced off the porch and into the bushes.

Seeing double, the hunter turned onto his back and saw a massive grizzly standing over him, the wind billowing around it like a great white wave. The bear was on its hind legs, standing so tall that its head ground against the ceiling, and it opened its maw with a roar. Absent his rifle and his head reeling from the blow, the hunter's only option was to wait out his fate—the railings on the porch barred all avenues of flight, and fighting back against such a beast would prove futile. The hunter recalled the doomed white mice of yesteryear as he remained frozen, aware that even the slightest movement could prove fatal.

The supine hunter and the upright bear stared at one another, both awaiting the next move of their adversary. Finally the bear groaned, almost as if annoyed, got back down on all fours, and walked away. After a time, during which the hunter held his throbbing head, he got up, grabbed his rifle from the bushes and returned to the cabin.

10
The Coldest Day

That's it. Today is the day, thought the hunter, as he rose from bed. He had been unable to sleep the remainder of the night, lying there wide-eyed, clutching his rifle for hours until the grey morning revealed itself from behind dusty curtains.

The hunter dressed warmly that day, for it was by far the coldest day yet. The freeze was so severe that he had spent the night both in his coat and under blankets, unable to defeat the chill with the modest remaining fire. When he went outside, the gale had subsided, but strong gusts remained and not once did they abate completely. Even with his deep, fur-lined hood, in which his face could barely be seen, the cold still fluttered along the tip of his nose. Any time his bare skin was exposed, say between a glove and a cuff of his sleeve, it stung as if cut by a razor.

Undeterred, the hunter grabbed an icepick from beneath the front seat of his truck and, for the final time, headed down to the lake.

The trek seemed longer that day, longer than any of

the days before, due in part to the cold but mostly due to the uncertainty of its conclusion. Would he be able to release the deer? Would the deer mortally injure itself while he attempted to free it? Would the wolves return to ravage their prey? Would he himself somehow become trapped on the ice? Nothing was certain.

The wind had picked up when at last the hunter arrived at the water's edge. As the sun rose in the sky the temperature oddly plummeted even further, as if an arctic chokehold had swept in to subdue the area.

The hunter looked down at the ice to find a slushy mire at the lake's edge. Today was the coldest day yet, how could it be that the lake was *less* frozen than before? Yet there it was, unfrozen, and the hunter followed the shore until he reached the deer…

…or where at least it had once been.

Hoof prints were visible leading out from the lake, despite the relentless wind, so they must have been fresh else they'd be gone. What was unmistakable, however, was the discolored snow, crimson and pink. While these evidenced injury, the limited blood at least suggested that the doe was not mortally wounded and its gait betrayed no broken bones. It might actually survive after all, the hunter thought.

For a moment he considered returning to his cabin and leaving the area altogether until the spring. Of all the outcomes he had predicted, a thawed surface and liberated deer was not one. And yet the hunter had to find the deer. He had to know how badly it was injured. He had to see how it was. After all this, he *had* to know, and the hoof prints and bloodstains in the snow were right there to guide him.

Back into the woods the hunter followed, the imprints becoming more distinct even as the amount of blood diminished. The deer's gashes must be drying out, or perhaps its open wounds were freezing over. And so the hunter followed, but always a step behind, always a little too slow.

At last the hunter paused. These woods seemed to go on forever. A yawning fog had befallen the area and the temperature continued to plunge. The hunter couldn't see more than a few yards into the distance and the cold was becoming so severe that he might not make it home if he did not begin anon.

As the hunter decided to forsake his pursuit, a boom rang out through the wilderness.

11
A Scarlet Testimony

He began to sprint, following the tracks again. He weaved and bobbed around the trees, tripping over roots and slipping on the snow. Finally he reached the end of the tracks and it was there at last he found the deer, on the ground, a bullet having pierced through its chest and out its side. Blood spurted out of the wound to the rhythm of its heartbeat, pooling cleanly beside its body and staining the tips of the hunter's boots.

Splayed in the snow, the doe looked up at the hunter with what seemed like recognition. It blinked every few seconds, each time slower than the last, and the hunter could see it would lie there for a long time before it bled out and succumbed.

The hunter raised his rifle and pointed it at the deer's head, thinking that this was something he should have done long ago. He had had several opportunities but never the will. Yet even now, with the doe in extremis, the hunter failed to pull the trigger—a failing due not to heartache, but to weakness—he was distracted by something unexpected in the snow.

Benjamin

Human footprints.

Human footprints stepped in blood.

Someone had shot the doe and walked up to admire their deed. Rather than finishing the kill and using it for fur, meat, a trophy or any other purpose, the gunman had left it to die alone, blinking and bleeding.

This the hunter refused to accept. He followed the bloody footprints until they delivered him to an unpaved road, their scarlet testimony halting where a new path began. Wide, colorless tire tracks had riven the powdery lane deep into the fog. And the hunter followed.

II. The Rising Son

*"For human wit is never so keen
As when the problem's unforeseen.
It's when the mind is most in fear
That guile and cunning first appear."*

-The Owl and the Nightingale
(author unknown)

12
Sins of the Father

Cast north from fertile grounds, Nahash came of age in the desperation of his flight. With each day north the days grew shorter, the shadows longer, until he at last succumbed to the corruption and frosted ruin of the hinterlands.

As a lone hunter banished from his pack, Nahash was not well fed, subsisting on what smaller prey he caught. When rabbits no longer appeared he resorted to mice, so small he could swallow them whole. Soon even the smallest prey he found no longer.

Famished and feeble, he one day came upon the scent of an elk, which, sensing the weakened wolf, stood its ground. Although guided by his instinct to back down from the beast, the rumbles in Nahash's belly created an urgency heretofore unknown to him. He carefully circled his prey before embarking on his first offensive. The animals collided and Nahash traded a kick to his chest for a laceration of the elk's hind leg. The elk shrieked as the red spray showered the rotting forest floor, and although it fled for miles, limping past the wasted trees, Nahash, gasping for air, followed its crimson trail until only the scent remained. The elk was found alive but drained on a bed of brown leaves and Nahash ate well that day.

In time Nahash entered the snow covered territory of a large pack, their many markings perfumed on crooked trunks. He knew that as a wolf alone he would stand no chance against a group of this size so he hid his own markings as well as he could. I should leave, he thought, for if the pack sees me as an intruder they will drive me away or worse. But he stayed, for despite the ongoing danger their lands were bountiful, and for many sunrises he survived stealthily along its fringes.

Nahash was content to remain veiled in the outskirts until he became impassioned by the scent of a female who had just, for the first time, bled. Then, on a night with no moon, Nahash found the alluring white wolf, Evanima, and knew the scent was hers. He stalked her until she was alone and then chased her deep into the woods. But he was faster than her, more powerful than her, and in time she could flee no longer and yielded to him before a wizened tree.

Her screams for help were heard by none, as the rest of the pack was far away and howling for her return.

13
The Ravine

When Evanima returned to her pack, Uranamo, the white bellied alpha with whom she met privately, smelled the crime that had been cast upon her.

"Who is this interloper I smell on your fur?" asked Uranamo, standing taller and broader than the other wolves.

"It is the snake Nahash, banished from his lands, unable to feed or breed without stealing that which belongs to others," Evanima replied. "He stalked me, he chased me, and I was forced to surrender to him."

"We must track down this reprobate Nahash," said Uranamo as he turned to the males of his pack, "for he is stealing our prey and taking our females."

And so the pack scoured their frozen lands seeking Nahash, but his scents were well hidden in the periphery. When no traces of him were found, the wolves ventured to the edges of their territory where they risked confrontations with neighboring packs. And in these fringes at last they found Nahash prowling in the shadows.

"Nahash!" shouted Uranamo, recognizing the offending scent.

Nahash knew he was caught so he stepped out from behind the trees. He pivoted his head from one side to another, assessing the hostile gathering before him.

"You have found me," said the drifter. "You needn't say anything more—I shall leave your lands at once."

"The time for that is over. Your lot has been cast," said Uranamo.

"My lot has been cast how? I scarcely did what I had to do to survive."

The wolves stared at him, not once breaking their gaze.

Nahash could see this wasn't going to be easy. "So it is then. What is it you want from me?"

Uranamo ignored the question and ordered his pack to surround and slay him. The wolves bared their teeth, growled, and encircled the trespasser. As the ring tightened, Nahash sprinted between two pack members and fled deeper into the woods and outside their lands. Fixated by their pursuit, the wolves followed Nahash, for despite their incursion into the adjacent territory, they knew these lands well too, so they chased him into a ravine where he could flee no longer. In a semi-circle the pack enclosed Nahash, who turned to face his pursuers, his back against a large black boulder.

"I yield! Show mercy and you shall not regret it. I will leave forthwith and never again shall you be affronted by my presence."

The pack waited for Uranamo to reaffirm the order.

Benjamin

"He dies," came the emotionless command.

Uranamo rushed in and went for his neck, but when Nahash turned to defend himself another wolf came from behind and tore a chunk of flesh from his hindquarters. Nahash tried to lunge forward but slipped on the blood gushing from his wound. When Uranamo pinned him down by the throat, with strength more overpowering than anything Nahash had ever felt, the rest of the wolves darted in and ripped him apart, piece by piece, limb by limb, organ by organ.

14
Spoils of Victory

Uranamo knew that, as the alpha, he must breed to maintain his position. Yet he suspected that he could have no children, as many attempts with females now deceased had yielded no fruit. In the pregnant Evanima he saw a potential for pups whom he could pass along as his should he take her as a wife. And she was the one female with whom this strategy would not enflame another male, for she was, as far as he knew, a maiden in the eyes of the others.

So when Uranamo returned to their lands he brought Evanima spoils from their victory as a ploy to woo her. She was not in their den so Uranamo followed her scent and found her curled under a bush.

"Evanima, I have brought you meat from our kill," said Uranamo, placing one of Nahash's avulsed legs on the ground before her.

"I am not hungry."

"You must eat."

"Really, I am fine."

"We know not when our next meal shall be."

Benjamin

"Thank you for your kindness, Uranamo, but give this meat to another for I am not interested in the consumption of my malefactor."

"I did not bring this meat for another. I brought it for you."

"And I thank you for that. But surely one of the pups must be hungry."

"The pups are fine, this meat was meant for you."

"Please Uranamo, I feel unwell. As you must know I am now with child."

"All the more reason to eat."

"Right now I just need some rest."

"Eat."

"Soon, Uranamo, soon.

"I shall not ask again."

"I don't understand why you are being like this," said Evanima, rising to her feet.

Uranamo grabbed Nahash's leg and pressed it against Evanima's mouth. When she did not take it from him, it fell on the ground before her.

"Uranamo... enough."

He picked up the leg and thrust it even harder into her face. She began to retreat.

"Uranamo, please!"

As she withdrew, Uranamo felt something from the depths ignite, a force from within that had been boiling throughout the encounter but had now run over. He grabbed her throat and pressed her face against the ground while positioning his own body behind her. He clutched her hips with his front paws, their barb-like claws digging into her flesh, and forced her down completely.

"Uranamo! Stop it! Enough! I'll eat."

But it was too late—Uranamo had come too far.

"No Uranamo, not again! I cannot bear for it to happen again…"

Ignoring her objections, Uranamo mounted Evanima, who quickly surrendered and sobbed throughout the horror. To these sounds the pack awoke, but their bellies were full so they closed their eyes and ears to the whimpers in the darkness.

15
The Nameless One

It is said that it is always darkest before the dawn, and yet there can be a rare moment when one's first light itself unleashes an even fuller blackness into the world. And so it was that day.

In the darkness of her womb there were three—two boys and a girl. Fortune shined upon Abaash, the grey one, for he was well positioned inside his mother and received the most nutrients. C'naal, the luckless black one, survived on whatever scraps remained after Abaash's gluttony. And the nameless one, who had no color at all, soon found herself absorbed by C'naal in his desperation for nourishment.

Throughout Evanima's pregnancy, the identity of the father the pack knew not. Both Nahash and Uranamo had forced themselves upon Evanima on those violent nights some two moons ago, and neither was sure to have won the struggle inside her. But true to his suspicions, Uranamo could have no natural children, so the battle between their seeds had been as one-sided as the one in which Nahash was slain.

And so came the day when Abaash and C'naal were expelled from Evanima and thrust into the light of the world. At Evanima's behest, Uranamo allowed the pups to live, for they were half hers, even though the pack knew at once that they were not of his blood for they bared the scent of the enemy. But both their lineage and the murder of their father were matters of which the pack would never speak, for they feared Uranamo's power and willingness to use it.

Although acting outwardly as if the pups were his, Uranamo knew in fact they were not so he cast them down where they were subordinated to all. Only once the pack had fed were the two brothers given a chance, and Abaash would seize the remnants for himself and grow to be strapping despite Uranamo's intentions.

C'naal, much like in the womb, was unable to compete with his larger brother and was left to pick the bones of whatever scraps remained, growing to be small and stunted. If C'naal tried to take some meat before Abaash had his fill, Abaash would hold him down by the throat, sometimes long after he submitted, but always past the point when blood had been drawn. His appetite was repeatedly left unfulfilled and he had to resort to cleverness rather than physicality to obtain much needed sustenance, sometimes either distracting Abaash or sneaking in to grab a small piece of meat while Abaash was muzzle-deep in a kill. Over time C'naal's corporeal shortcomings were far surpassed by the cunning he was forced to nurture to survive his brother.

While Abaash, being simple, had never given their

predicament much thought, C'naal always wondered why they, the purported sons of the alpha, had been relegated to the bottom of the hierarchy. Through his canny, C'naal soon realized that their ongoing plight was a consequence of Uranamo's vindictiveness. He discovered that not only had they no relation to the alpha but also that it may have been Uranamo himself who was responsible for the death of their father. Although the pack dared not speak of such affairs, C'naal was able to infer much from the unsaid, and he would, for many moons, harbor a silent resentment towards Uranamo, believing that the day would come when he could use this information for his own gain. Abaash, meanwhile, was oblivious to their sordid pedigree, since C'naal had no intention of sharing this secret knowledge with an abusive brother who would have freely allowed him to starve.

Abaash continued to strengthen, and the pack soon found him to be a valuable member who played vital roles in rushing and taking down prey. C'naal, meanwhile, used his acuity to more effectively track prey, and even learned how to predict where scents might first be found. But only Abaash's physicality in the kill was noticed by the others, and C'naal's contributions were barely recognized. With his improved standing, Abaash would soon realize that he no longer had to be subjugated by the others, and the pack would never be the same.

16
Philo and the Elk

On a late winter morning, the pup Philo begged his mother to let him join the hunt. But he was only a few months old and too small, so his mother commanded him to remain in the den with the other pups. Once the pack had left though, Philo's curiosity would prevail and he followed them from far behind.

Later that day, the pack followed the scent of an elk until they found it chewing bark in the shade of a broken tree. As the pack approached, Uranamo, standing first before the other wolves, signaled some to each side and others to the back to surround their prey. As the circle of wolves emerged from behind the trees, the elk refused to surrender, and Philo would watch the forthcoming encounter from the shadows.

Each wolf took turns feinting to provoke the elk to flight, but every time it stood its ground, slamming its hooves into the snow in defiance. The pack was too hungry to abandon their hard found quarry, so they took turns rushing and trying to bite it. Each attempt failed, until even the mighty Uranamo, now older but still clinging to power, was staggered by a kick to the chest. While Uranamo gasped for air, Abaash, on his first attempt, managed to bite and lacerate the elk's hind leg. He leapt back with a satisfied face full of blood and glared directly at Uranamo with eyes open wide. Under normal circumstances Uranamo would have stamped out this challenge at once, but he was still recovering from the blow. The elk bolted as soon as it was bitten so the pack didn't notice Uranamo's reluctance to engage.

The elk galloped straight towards Philo, its footfalls buffeting the ground. The pup could only cringe upon the beast's rapid approach, for there was no time to flee. The elk trampled Philo, who was lifted in a cloud of snow and debris. The pup landed on a pile of rocks, his ribs pummeled.

Only C'naal, who was too feeble to contribute much to the kill, heard the muted whines from afar and saw Philo limping in the bushes. The pup was battered but appeared to have somehow avoided any mortal wounds. And so C'naal, who was used to eating but meager portions, forwent his meal, grabbed the wounded pup by the scruff of the neck and carried him back to the den. He set Philo in a warm compartment with the other pups and made him a soft bed of leaves to lie on.

When the pack returned, Philo's mother saw his wounds and ran to him. She saw that although bruised he would over time heal and survive the trauma. She didn't understand how he could have come to be in this condition. Philo, however, admitted his disobedience and how he had suffered in consequence. He also told her and the rest of the wolves of C'naal's heroism, and C'naal that day would be praised and respected by the pack for the first time.

While C'naal was in the den, humbled by the unexpected praise, he saw Uranamo's broad silhouette standing the entryway. He met eyes with the alpha and the pack grew silent, thinking he would enter and offer him thanks as well. But the tall wolf instead turned and peered at Abaash, then back at C'naal, and then walked out into the forest, saying but a word.

17
The Venom of Time

Uranamo could feel the venom of time beating down on his bones. Each hunt grew harder, each assertion of dominance more painful, and rising from slumber bore new challenges and threats with each passing day.

He saw that Abaash continued to rise through the hierarchy by means of brute force and willpower. Abaash habitually failed to offer him deference, and far too often did he behave with an etiquette unbefitting social norms. C'naal, meanwhile, was a small, submissive wolf who generally kept to himself—he had no social status of which to speak, even after saving Philo, and posed no physical danger. But perhaps most importantly, he despised his brother—Uranamo's greatest threat. C'naal therefore seemed a fitting instrument for Uranamo's nascent defense plan, but he had to approach it thoughtfully, for not only would he be pitting brother against brother, he would be doing so while presenting himself as their father.

"You, C'naal, have a sight belonging to no other,"

said Uranamo, as they walked through the forest. "Your tracking instincts and ability to predict the movements of game are unsurpassed."

"Thank you."

"Today I find myself in a dark place, C'naal. I seem to face the same horrible choice as my mother once before me."

"I know nothing of her."

Uranamo stared at C'naal, wanting to continue, but was unable to speak until taking a deep breath and collecting himself.

"I will now tell you a tale none alive have heard, and long gone are all who bore witness. It is a tale I struggle to repress into the deepest reaches of my memory, but can nevertheless recall every detail as if it happened but moments ago."

C'naal nodded even though he was unsure where Uranamo was going with this.

"You are probably unaware that I once had a twin," began Uranamo. "When we were pups, a few weeks old at most, our pack one day came upon a herd of caribou. I stood at the crest of a hill with my brother, in awe at the sight of the herd which stretched across the valley and beyond, a gathering of prey far larger than either of us could ever dream.

"My brother and I were told to stay back, so we watched from behind as our elders descended into the valley. The caribou continued to forage, seemingly oblivious until it was too late, and our leader rushed in and took one down singlehandedly.

"At this sudden commotion, the caribou did notice—all at once—that they were under attack. My brother and I marveled at how, in their panic, the herd seemed to move as a single organism—almost as if each animal was but a particle in a river of prey.

"Our amazement though became terror when the herd unexpectedly turned and raced up the hill towards us. Although we recognized at once our peril, so untried were we that we froze when the caribou unwittingly charged our way. Not that there was much, at that point, we could have done to escape. The herd, perhaps numbering in the thousands, ran over my brother and me, and we suffered a trampling that seemed to never end.

"When at last the dust cleared, I rose—quite damaged but still somehow able to stand. I know not how I survived, or how I had been so lucky as to suffer no permanent wounds.

"After some time I located my brother, who, although still alive, had both hind legs crushed and blackened from being pulverized into the dirt by a thousand hooves. He tried to crawl towards me, crying for help and gasping for air, his front paws dragging the rest of his limp, mangled carcass behind him.

"My mother wept upon sight of her crippled son, but soon said to me coldly, 'Let's go'. I implored her to take him with us, but she refused on grounds that he was ruined and would be but an impediment to us all. 'Please Mommy, don't go! Mommy, no!' my brother begged, and I, in turn, begged with him. But my mother hoisted me by the back of the neck and carried me away, affording me no chance to remain by his side. I watched my brother try to catch up, his eyes wide in desperation and panic from being abandoned by his mother before his very eyes. But with only two front paws and dragging so much dead weight behind him, he quickly fell behind and none of the other wolves even bothered to look his way.

"As the distance between us grew, he continued pleading from afar, screaming over and over 'Mommy, come back! Mommy, I'll be good...', but to no avail. Soon we were far enough that his cries were drowned out by the wind sweeping through the valley. I craned my neck, hoping to at least glimpse him one last time, but the space between us was now clouded by the fog."

"So you, I suppose, were the lucky brother," said C'naal, disguising his resentment.

Uranamo stopped for a moment and sighed, peering down into the snow. "I guess I was lucky in a lot of ways that day." After a long pause he lifted his head and with a countenance of gravity turned once more to C'naal.

"Do you know why I told you this tale?"

"No."

"What matters, above all, is *the pack*. Do you agree?"

"Yes, but why..."

"My mother knew she had to sacrifice her son for the pack's well-being."

"He would have died anyway."

"Probably, but we'll never know. Perhaps he could have lived out his life as a cripple."

"A cripple that would have been but a weakness for others to carry."

"Exactly. But my mother would have had her son."

"That is unrealistic. She did what had to be done."

"So you agree then, that the pack matters above all—that our combined welfare should be put above that of any single wolf, regardless of one's relation to that wolf?"

"Yes, I suppose I do."

"You have proven me correct, C'naal. Not only have you the sharpest mind in the pack, but you also recognize the hard decisions we must sometimes make to navigate through our treacherous world."

"Yes, but—"

"More impressive, however, is the fact that you have foresight; a talent made evident by your ability to predict, in a hunt, where scents might first be found. And by extension, an ability that must also include sensing threats before they arise."

"What does this have to do—"

"You see the world for what it truly is, C'naal. You see things others do not see. And you surely see that your brother is now grown and will one day try to unseat me."

The black wolf could finally see where this was going, and after a long pause, assented. "It wouldn't come as a surprise."

"Indeed. And you must also recognize that his attempts will divide the pack and imperil us all."

"Perhaps."

"While Abaash may be physically strong, he is also simple and lacks the finesse required to be a pack leader."

"He is lacking in certain qualities, I agree."

"You see then how you now find yourself at a

crossroads."

"How so?"

"You sense a threat, as I do, to the collective."

"Meaning that the pack would be worse off if Abaash were to replace you?"

"Far worse off. Endangered, in fact. You see this, surely. And so it is you now have a choice. Align with me; use your mind to help me strategize against your brother. Or betray me, and tell Abaash of the plot against him."

"And you want an answer now."

Uranamo didn't respond, nor did he need to. C'naal knew he had no choice; he now stood alone with a powerful, violent wolf. Rejecting his alliance now would be far too dangerous.

"Then my answer is yes. You have my word. I will support you."

"Excellent," said Uranamo. "I need you to go back and think. Consider how we can achieve this with the least blood spilt. I would rather banish than kill him, at least out of respect for your mother."

"Banishing him might not be as easy as you think. Abaash is the type of wolf who will fight to the death and take many down with him."

"All the more reason I need a formidable plan. The path forward is not simple."

"I see."

"But be not mistaken. Should my hand be forced, I will not hesitate to bring his life to an end."

"I never suspected you would."

"You understand the task at hand then?"

"I do."

"Good. Soon comes the next full moon. At eventide, you and I shall meet to decide Abaash's fate. Together, we will save the pack from this growing menace."

"But why me? Surely there are others more suitable for the task."

"Physically, perhaps—but I have plenty of other wolves to use as force. It is your mind I need here, C'naal, not your body."

"Yes but even so, no one will listen to me no matter how great a plan I devise."

Uranamo narrowed his eyes. "You think that what you did yesterday went unnoticed by the others?"

"What do you mean?"

"Your savvy and compassion have always been clear to me, but it was demonstrated to all when you alone saw one of our young trampled. Even Philo's mother neglected to notice what had occurred."

"But she was in the middle of the hunt and couldn't have even known he was there."

"Nonetheless, if not for you, Philo might have died alone in the wilderness."

"I did only what was right."

"What you did struck me quite hard, given what I had experienced long ago."

"Still I contend that I did only what needed to be done."

"Perhaps. But your stock rose; you are no longer just a hanger-on in the eyes of the others. You have earned their respect."

"Yes but—"

"Believe you this—with your cunning plan, and my backing, we will succeed."

C'naal exhaled—there was no point in arguing further. "Alright then. On the next full moon we'll meet."

Uranamo suspected a hidden reticence in C'naal's tone, so he glared into his eyes to remind him that there would be consequences for duplicity. "Remember—my choice today is identical to the one faced by my mother many moons ago. A *son* for the good of the pack. It was a decision that had to be made; you said it yourself. It was no truer then than it is today."

"Yes. The path forward is clear."

Uranamo appraised C'naal's bearing and sensed no uncertainty this time. As he began to walk away, C'naal followed, but the old wolf ordered him to wait, for he did not want to risk Abaash seeing them return alongside one another.

And so it was that C'naal found himself alone in the woods with his thoughts, Uranamo failing to realize that the clever wolf's decision was far from settled. His commitment to Uranamo had been made under duress, so he risked losing no honor by betraying him. But which side to take? The oppressive alpha who murdered his father or the cruel brother whose selfishness had weakened him since birth? C'naal indeed stood at a crossroads, with the pack's future in the balance.

18
His Time Cometh

While at first C'naal had agreed to join the conspiracy, what Uranamo did not realize is that the clever wolf always knew he was not of his blood, and he hated Uranamo for killing his father and relegating him and his brother to the bottom of the pack. In a sense, Uranamo was even more responsible for C'naal's enduring malnourishment than was his own brother. Plus, Uranamo always stood by in silence when Abaash would abuse him, and C'naal resented that only now, when Uranamo sensed a threat, would he acknowledge C'naal's contributions to the pack's well-being. While C'naal objected to Uranamo's use of such a heartbreaking tale to segue into his true objectives, perhaps what disturbed him most were the parallels drawn from this tale as if Uranamo was truly his father. C'naal indeed saw the world for what it was, as the old wolf had said, and after much reflection, he decided to betray Uranamo and tell Abaash of both the plotted treachery and their secret origin.

Given his brother's penchant for aggression towards him, C'naal had to tread carefully. The knowledge he would soon convey dealt with a delicate matter and the clever wolf knew not what his reaction might be. Abaash, being the slower of the two brothers, might be easily persuaded. But this ignorance might also prevent him from seeing the veracity in C'naal's words, and construe his motives for something they were not.

"Abaash, we must speak," began C'naal, having pulled him away from the other wolves.

Abaash had little patience for his smaller brother. "What could we possibly have to speak about?"

"We must speak about our father."

"Fuck our father."

"Why would you say such a thing? The man of whom you speak is our leader."

"I don't need lessons about the hierarchy from the likes of you."

"Then why such hatred?"

"If he had his way, I would be but an accursed, stunted wolf like you."

"And yet you are not. Why do you think he has tried to consign us, his supposed sons, to the lowest caste?"

"His reasons matter not."

"But they do, Abaash. The reasons matter."

"Get to the point. I do not have all day."

"Think about it, Abaash. In what world does a leader relegate his own children to eat but remnants of kills? In what world does the leader not insist his pups eat first before those of other wolves?"

"I do not know and I do not care."

"Listen to me for once!"

Benjamin

Abaash took a step towards C'naal, who bent his ears back and crouched in submission. "Again I say get to the point" said the larger wolf.

"The answer, Abaash, is that no leader would do that to his children."

"Our father must be the exception then," said Abaash, starting to walk away.

C'naal knew that his brother's little patience had worn out and he had to strike now or never strike at all. "But we are not his children," he blurted.

Abaash stopped cold, his back to C'naal. "What do you mean, 'we are not his children'?"

"I mean exactly that. Uranamo is not our father."

"I've heard enough of this," said Abaash, now storming away.

"Abaash, stop, get back here!" said C'naal, gently gripping Abaash's hind leg with his teeth to halt his departure. Abaash turned, incensed by this boldness, but did not attack after seeing the mien of urgency upon his brother's face.

"My brother, listen to me," continued the clever wolf, "it is something I have always suspected. I have, for many sunrises, listened closely to what others say, things said in passing, secrets spoken only below one's breath. These whispers all lead to the same conclusion—Uranamo is not our father."

"If not him then who?"

"I don't know, but Uranamo must have killed whoever it was long ago."

"Why?"

"So that he could pass us off as his own, I suppose."

"Have you asked our mother about this?"

"No, for fear that Uranamo might uncover my insights."

"I've heard enough of this nonsense."

"Fine. Believe me or don't, it matters not to me."

"Then why bother me with your stories?"

"By understanding our history you will better recognize what is to come."

"History is of no importance to me."

"Perhaps not. But what should be of paramount importance to you is the violence about to befall you."

Abaash's eyes widened. "Violence?"

"Uranamo is plotting to banish you."

"Ha! Let him try."

"This is a whole conspiracy I speak of."

"Another one of your theories?"

"Did you see us walk into the woods yesterday?"

"No."

"Well we did, Uranamo invited me to walk alone with him into the woods, and when we were far from the others, as you and I are now, he solicited my help in a plot against you."

"Did he?"

"He did."

"Why should I believe you?"

"How would I benefit from telling such tales?"

"What could an ungainly rat-wolf like you possibly offer him?"

"He has asked me to come up with the plan."

"Because you are just *so* smart."

"That's not what I'm saying—I'm trying to warn you. Don't you see what's going on here?"

"I need no warning. Let him try. I can handle Uranamo myself."

"It won't be just him."

Abaash tilted his head. "Perhaps it is *you* who is setting me up."

"Setting you up how? Think about it. Uranamo is old. His time cometh soon. If not by you then by another wolf. He cannot lead forever."

"True."

"You and I have always had our differences, Abaash. And yet you are my brother. I cannot just stand by and allow this imposter to banish you—or worse."

Abaash stopped and looked away for a moment, staring into the forest. C'naal could see that he was thinking—simple thoughts perhaps, but thoughts nonetheless. After a time, Abaash turned back towards C'naal and replied, his voice hesitating, his voice low.

"The other day when that idiot pup was trampled, after I opened the elk's leg and was covered in its blood—I could have taken Uranamo then and there."

"Indeed you could have taken him. He was reeling in the snow."

"And yet I did not, I decided instead to chase the elk with the others. Do you know why I did not take him then, while he was incapacitated?"

"No."

"Because I can take him any time I want. His time is

done. The wolf is old."

"Perhaps, Abaash, perhaps. But you are wrong to think you can take him any time. Once he gathers the strength of the pack against you, you will not stand a chance. One wolf cannot defeat many."

"And if your tale of treachery is but a lie?"

"So what of it? Once you unseat him, the leadership will be yours."

"The leadership will be mine indeed. I *can* take him."

C'naal could see his words were finally affecting his larger brother. Abaash's tone had changed—he no longer snapped back impetuously; his responses emerged more slowly, more thoughtfully. Just a little more push and C'naal might achieve his goal.

"And you can do it now, Abaash. Why take a chance and wait? You are stronger than he. Time has been cruel to him. The time for a new leader is now. That wolf is you."

"And what do you get out of all this?"

"I get nothing. But I no longer have to pledge fealty to a fraud who I believe killed our father and whom I hate; a charlatan whose only meaningful interaction with me was to plot against you. Should he rid the pack of you how do I know what my own fate will be? He has no fondness for me in his heart. In his eyes, I am but a tool."

"I don't know. Still something seems amiss."

"There is nothing amiss, Abaash. Not from me, at least. You say you can take Uranamo now. I agree. Whether or not my stories of intrigue are true, why take the chance? Who knows what the future holds? Your best opportunity to overturn him is now."

"And if I wait?"

"By waiting, you risk that what I say is true and he, perhaps even as we speak, gathers the legions against you."

After another thoughtful silence, Abaash finally broke. "So it is then."

"So it is," agreed the clever wolf.

19
A Silent Message

And so came the eve of a waxing moon when Abaash rose up and bared his teeth against Uranamo. Although timeworn and broken down, Uranamo was larger, broader chested, and battle seasoned from the many threats over time to his authority. The two wolves clashed that day—their muzzles stained with blood, their bodies tattered with ripped fur. But Abaash's tenacity and youth proved to be too much for the aging Uranamo, who soon found himself belly up in submission.

"Kill me now," said Uranamo, "for I am an old and battered wolf who has finally been overthrown." But Abaash was unsatisfied with a mere victory, and wanted to deliver a warning to all the other wolves, so he took Uranamo into his mouth and eviscerated him. As Abaash's maw dripped the gore of mutilation, Uranamo, relieved of his manhood, limped away from the pack forever, leaving nothing but a red trail in the snow as memory of his humiliation.

Disappearing into the forest, Uranamo turned one

last time and locked eyes with C'naal, almost as if relaying a silent message he expected him to understand. But C'naal knew not Uranamo's cryptic expression—perhaps he was acknowledging C'naal's betrayal, or perhaps he was simply conveying the sorrow of being torn from his brethren forevermore. Then again, perhaps it was neither—simply a blank gaze from a fallen leader that C'naal happened to receive. Whatever the case, C'naal would never answer this mystery, for neither he, nor any other wolf, would ever lay eyes upon Uranamo again.

20
Winter Ticks

Abaash was a strong leader whose reign proved bountiful for all. Even the feeble C'naal, who was used to eating poorly, would find himself well-nourished under Abaash's leadership. The woods teemed with deer, the elk were plentiful, and no rival packs or bears surfaced as competition. No detractors to his command arose since the wolves enjoyed each day with high morale and bursting bellies.

But what the pack did not realize at first was that Abaash had nothing to do with the surplus of game; he had simply been the recipient of good fortune and the timing of herd movements. So when, one terrible winter, the pack suffered a dearth of prey they began to starve, and Abaash's simplemindedness would be exposed by his inability to adapt. Everyone, even Abaash, became so frail and gaunt that when a family of deer finally came through their lands the wolves were unable to catch even the weak or the old.

The next night, Abaash embarked alone into the wilderness, knowing that to maintain his authority he must find a food source for his suffering pack. He crossed snow covered hills, dead forests, and lakes of ice. While his thick fur helped fight off the stinging cold, his face quickly became covered with chunks of snow that clung to him like leeches. He scraped the snow with his paws but this only flattened the clumps and pressed them more firmly against his snout. Again and again he considered returning to the warm den, where at least he would not risk dying alone, but onward he marched, knowing that he and the rest of the pack must feed. After days of searching, he at last came upon an ailing moose, and when Abaash returned to the den, he instructed that the pack seek it out before it was found by others.

Following a lengthy passage, the wolves came upon the moose whose skeletal chest thrust up and down rapidly beneath a brittle layer of skin. The moose was splayed on a bed of putrid twigs, their brown and grey tips protruding upwards from the snow. Its flaccid, frost-bitten ears hung on the sides of its head and its eyes peered unblinking at the dead branches above.

At first this moose appeared to be the perfect catch; dying and unable to fight back or flee. But as the pack drew closer, they paused aghast for the moose's fur was covered with pallid blotches where hordes of tiny brown insects hung, bleeding the beast. These insects clung to its belly, they clung to its rear. They clung to its ears, to its legs, and to its back. The pestilence crawled on the ground around the moose, creeping into its snout, into its mouth, into its anus. There must have been a million of these creatures, and it was at times hard to tell where the swarm ended and the moose began.

As C'naal studied the dying moose, he imagined the anguish it must have endured while being slowly drained, and for a moment he actually pitied the creature they had come to slay. He envisioned the animal in an awkward gait, scraping its body against the trees to relieve the irritation. He imagined it faltering until it no longer had the strength to even stand, finally reaching its inescapable destiny—lying in the filthy snow, consumed in a prolonged demise. C'naal saw that before him stood a fate far worse than starvation, a fate more gruesome and unbearable than anything he could have imagined. In spite of his fear of his larger brother, he could not help but speak against the folly of what was about to pass.

"Approach no further," C'naal cried out, as the sun broke above the horizon like a bleeding eye. "For this blight is one that will infect us all."

"Listen not to my brother," said Abaash, stunned at C'naal's effrontery, "for we must eat lest soon we die this dreadful winter."

"Fool, you have led us to an accursed beast whose disease will condemn us all, including our young, to a life of affliction. We need a new strategy to survive, for scavenging our lands has proven to be in vain."

"We eat what we find," growled the stubborn Abaash. "That has always been the way. There is no other way."

Heartbroken from seeing their hopes for food dashed, the wolves were tempted to obey Abaash's perilous command. None, however, proved willing to come close to the infested moose, for they saw the wisdom in C'naal's words.

Abaash, who had suffered in his quest to find nourishment for all, assessed the pack and saw they obeyed his brother instead of he. Enraged by their insubordination, he clutched the black wolf by his muzzle and held him down. C'naal jerked and flailed, trying to break free, struggling to shift his smothered snout out of his brother's maw. The pack screamed for Abaash to let go while C'naal went belly up, his paws flapping in the air until going limp.

"You all do what you must, but today I feed," roared Abaash as he dropped his brother and turned towards the moose. Although no wolf alone had the courage to stymie his advance, together they stepped before Abaash and forbade him to feed for they knew he would bring the contagion back to the den for all to suffer. Abaash bared his teeth and repeatedly sought to pierce the barrier created by his brethren, but every time was thwarted, so he stormed away and became lost among the trees.

As the wolf's shadow merged into the black forest, the pack helped C'naal return to consciousness. When he awoke, he felt as if his days were numbered. Speaking out against his brother, especially in front of the others, would not be soon forgotten. And to make matters worse, the other wolves had disobeyed Abaash as a consequence of this outburst and then stepped in to support C'naal.

C'naal knew he must act soon, for not only was the pack's survival threatened by the lack of game and his brother's incompetence, but now C'naal was personally threatened by his wrath. If only he had foreseen this, and not betrayed Uranamo long before—but who could have predicted the desolation cast upon them all?

If he were to somehow outlast the famine, could he also survive his brother's coming storm? He had to find a way out—a shield against his brother, an escape from the want, some cunning answer to it all. But what, indeed, could the clever wolf do against such odds?

21
The Cabin

And so the pack continued to starve. The pups were the first to fall, then the old. The dead would be consumed by the living—children by their mothers, parents by their young. Even the beautiful Evanima would fall, with C'naal being left to chew her bones after Abaash gorged himself upon her flesh. Yet this was inadequate for the pack's survival, so their ribs protruded from their chests, their legs were frail, and their paws shuddered with every step.

Abaash continued to scour their lands, sometimes alone, sometimes leading groups of other wolves, but not once did he detect any scents in the barren woods. C'naal, meanwhile, recognized that the pack's despair could only be solved by unusual means since the *status quo* no longer proved effective. So C'naal ventured alone beyond the borders of their lands, into the treacherous territories of rival packs, past a lake of ice, and down a long, winding path until he heard an unfamiliar humming in the distance. He followed the sound to a clearing at the end of which stood a decrepit cabin.

C'naal climbed a few steps up to the structure, the boards creaking beneath every footfall. At the top of the stairs was a landing that was empty save a pile of mutilated trees and a strange container filled with ice water. The container smelled of something unnatural, as if it had been constructed from a material not of this world. The water itself, however, seemed normal, so C'naal paused for a moment to drink.

A doorway stood at the center of the landing. C'naal approached it slowly for he knew not what might lie beyond. He stopped to sniff under the door and although unusual scents abounded none were strong enough to evidence the immediate presence of another entity. C'naal pushed the door open with his muzzle and entered the cabin.

True to C'naal's suspicions, the structure was vacant, but it seemed to be recently occupied by a creature whose scent was unknown to him. Something in the air though gave him the sense that he stood in the den of a dangerous being, something far more terrifying than perhaps he could ever understand, a presence whose path he might be destined to one day cross.

Desperate and starved, C'naal perused the cabin and found several blankets strewn beside an ash-filled alcove along with a noxious glass bottle. Finding nothing of use, he sniffed the air again and caught a faint scent of deer which led him to a large, rectangular metal box along the wall. C'naal poked and clawed at the box but it refused to budge.

He stepped back to examine the structure as if it was

a riddle. There should be a way in. There had to be a way in. The box however was featureless save a hooked metal bar hanging from its front. That must be the key, C'naal thought, so he stood on his hind legs and took the metal into his mouth. When he pulled back, the box sprung open with little effort.

The frozen air pouring from the box was strangely warmer than the air outside. The box was full of raw deer meat, cut and stored by some advanced method. Never before had C'naal seen meat so delicately sliced. He ate a large chunk, chomping through the frozen cut, while behind him the box almost seemed to close itself.

C'naal returned to his pack and waited until Abaash had fallen asleep. He gathered the wolves and told them that he had found reprieve from their suffering and that they must go on without Abaash, their failed leader, for he might stop them in an effort to thwart his brother. C'naal reminded them that Abaash was the one who had led them to the infested moose and had been prepared to bring the affliction back to their den and doom them all. He reminded them how Abaash listened to no one and was unwilling to consider any hunting strategies save the ones continuing to prove fruitless this awful winter. All of these things the pack understood, so they left Abaash asleep and alone and they followed C'naal into the wilderness.

At the fringes of their territory, the pack hesitated, but they trusted C'naal, and they believed he had found deliverance from their torment. So they continued forth, in time reaching the sinuous dirt road where they heard the humming in the distance. "This is the sound of our salvation" C'naal told the others. So they entered the cabin, overturned the metal box, and ate until their bellies were full.

When at last the pack emerged from the dark interior, C'naal stood first before the other wolves. As he advanced into the forest, the pack followed in steps that seemed so natural behind their unlikely savior.

22
A Wolf Apart

When Abaash awoke, he was a wolf apart. The den had been deserted by the others who had silently left him in the night. He didn't know why he had been forsaken, but the pack's scent was fresh and he could follow it with ease.

Abaash followed the scent to the boundary of their lands where he heard the howling of unfamiliar, faraway voices. With trepidation he continued forth into the alien territory, seeking his pack and seeking reasons for his abandonment.

Soon he reached the edge of a ravine, and in the distance he saw many wolves approaching from along the rim. The group radiated with an energy he had not seen in a fortnight—their steps were sure and their heads held high. Abaash paused, thinking at first that this must be a rival pack, but as they advanced he saw they were in fact his kin when he recognized C'naal leading the rest of the wolves.

"Where have you gone and why have you ventured asunder without your leader?" Abaash bellowed as he came face-to-face with the others.

"We have abandoned you, Abaash, for your leadership has failed us," replied C'naal. "Under your command our pack has lost many members and turned sickly."

"Silence, runt," growled the larger brother, who smelled the raw deer meat, "and lead me to your kill or I shall destroy you once and for all. I am your leader and you will submit."

"No, brother. *I* am the leader now."

Abaash glared at C'naal with eyes wide open, neck arched, tail held high, and ears bent forward. His panting quickened and his misty breath drifted over his scrawny, undersized brother. After a moment he charged C'naal, grabbed him by the throat and flung him to the precipice of the ravine. Injured but alive, C'naal slowly stood on shaking legs.

"This is your last chance, brother," said Abaash as he calmly closed the distance.

C'naal bled profusely but his wounds were not mortal. He scanned the wolves to see who, if any, would be willing to step in before his fuming brother. Almost instantly, the other males charged Abaash and took him down. Abaash fought back, and drew the blood of many, but the combined strength of the pack was too much for even he. Abaash would never submit, but soon found himself unable to rise on his shredded legs.

C'naal looked down upon his dying brother, a torrent of emotions running through his mind. Here he was—his own sibling, the wolf with whom he shared his mother's womb—but also the wolf who had menaced him since childhood and condemned him to be the scrawny, disadvantaged wolf that he came to be. Despite all this, C'naal had done so much to support him—he had betrayed Uranamo, saved Abaash from exile, and inspired him to seize the leadership for himself—only to later regret everything when imperiled by his wrath. Through these conflicting feelings C'naal saw though, in the end, only sadness and lament—not for what he had endured, but because of the inevitability of what came next.

And so, with teeth clenched, C'naal braced himself and pushed Abaash into the ravine. His dying carcass bounced off the cliff sides, its torn flesh thumping along the walls and landing with a thud beside a large black boulder. Abaash looked up to see the silhouettes of the pack staring down at him from the ravine's edge. As they turned for the last time, so did he, and with his dying breath Abaash bared his teeth when he saw beside him the skull of a long dead wolf, and then closed his eyes forever.

interlude:
Van Diemen's Land

23
Bounties

The tragic tale of the thylacine is difficult to convey without an impression of hyperbole. It is the story of a truly unique creature who became the victim of a systematic extermination followed by years of neglect and abandonment. Despite its importance, it is a story far too few have heard.

Thylacines, or Tasmanian Tigers, were the last members of the family *Thylacinidae* dating back about 20 million years. They were carnivorous marsupials that once roamed Australia, New Guinea and Tasmania. It is believed these 3 landmasses were once a single continent until about 10,000 years ago when the last ice age ended, flooding the lowlands and imprisoning the populations onto individual islands.

Adult thylacines stood about 2 feet tall at the shoulder, were 4 to 6 feet long, and weighed up to 70 pounds. They were quadrupedal, looking somewhat like large canines, with short brown fur and 20 or so black stripes from their mid-back to the start of their tail. It is for these stripes that they were given the nickname *tigers*, although contemporaneous Tasmanians also sometimes called them *wolves* or *hyenas*. In reality, thylacines were closely related to none of these animals.

Although little documentation of the thylacine's behavior remains, it is known that they were nocturnal, and their stripes suggested camouflaging or other hunting benefits in the woodland. As marsupials, mothers would nurture their pups in a pouch and continue to protect them for some time after. They had defined home ranges of about 25 square miles but did not appear to be territorial. Although given a reputation of fierceness, perhaps due to their massive jaws capable of opening up to 90 degrees, most observers agreed that the animal was shy.

The thylacine was exclusively carnivorous and hunted an array of fauna including wombats, birds and other small animals. Its favorite meal however appeared to be the Tasmanian emu, a large flightless bird whose disappearance, a consequence mostly of habitat destruction by humans, may have been associated with that of the thylacine. With the extinction of the emu, thylacines started targeting poultry and sheep farms for sustenance.

Subfossil bone records indicate that thylacines disappeared from mainland Australia about 2,000 years ago and from New Guinea well before then. This disappearance has been attributed to a variety of factors including lack of genetic diversity, disease, loss of habitat, and competition with invasive dingoes. Mostly, however, it is believed to be the fault of humans, whose environmental fury resulted in the extinction of 90% of Australia's vertebrates in the millennia following their arrival. And yet the thylacine somehow persisted in the relatively small, isolated island of Tasmania for some time after.

When Tasmania was first settled by the British around 1800, thylacines existed in heaviest distributions in the northern parts of the island, their population totaling somewhere in the 5,000 range. Their numbers began to rapidly decline due to both habitat destruction and competition from feral dogs that had been introduced by settlers. Although rarely seen by people, thylacines became regarded as pests and settlers routinely hunted them down. Farmers and shepherds, seeking to end the decimation of their flocks, would set up traps to kill them. This was just the beginning of what would ultimately turn into one of the most ignominious ecological witch hunts in history, when numerous, well-publicized attacks on sheep and poultry farms for which thylacines received credit resulted in their systematic genocide.

The first bounties for dead thylacines were introduced in 1830 by a group of wealthy London merchants called The Van Diemen's Land Company, whose investments in sheep farms were under financial distress. These were followed by decades of government sponsored eradication until the species became critically endangered. Different bounties were awarded for adults and pups, the latter of which were typically slaughtered in groups of 2 to 4. Between 1888 and 1909, a total of 2,184 government bounties were awarded for dead thylacines, although this figure is thought by many to be fewer than the actual number slain, since farmers, who had no formal record-keeping process, commonly paid larger bounties than the government.

By 1920 almost no thylacines remained in the wild, but due to potentially profitable demand from overseas collectors, the Tasmanian government in 1928 reversed its focus from annihilation to conservation of the species, and in fact proposed the creation of nature reserves in the western parts of the island. But it was far too late, and the last thylacine known to be killed in the wild was shot in 1930 by the farmer Wilfred Batty who had observed it roaming around his home for several weeks. A photograph, in which Batty grins beside the corpse of his victim, remains as evidence of his butchery.

If some irony can be drawn from all this, it appears, with the benefit of hindsight, that thylacines were not even responsible for many of the attacks on livestock; they had been carried out by feral dogs or dingoes. This argument would be strengthened when it was revealed, many years later, that most photographs of thylacines running off with dead chickens had been staged—using either thylacines already in captivity or cadavers that had been mounted and posed by photographers.

Nevertheless, due to the chain of events that followed the misperceptions and propaganda, fate had been sealed. The last thylacine in captivity, commonly referred to as *Benjamin*, was snared in the Florentine Valley in 1933 by a trapper named Elias Churchill. Benjamin was shipped in a cramped, lightless cargo train to the Beaumaris Zoo in Hobart, where it would go on to live for 3 years. Scarred on its hind paw from a violent snaring, it spent the remainder of its life in a small fenced-in cage

Benjamin

with a concrete floor, quarters as dissimilar to its natural habitat as can be imagined. Grainy black and white films remain of the creature, in which it yawns, lies around, sniffs its surroundings, and paces back and forth incessantly. Many of its behaviors mimic that of a common pet dog. Later examinations of these films indicate that, based on both anatomy and behavior, "Benjamin" was actually female.

The 1936 Hobart winter was especially terrible, with temperatures, rain, and snow all being severe. The Beaumaris Zoo was understaffed due to the effects of the Great Depression, and many of the zoo's prized exhibits ended up underfed and ignored. Many animals were frequently left out in the cold, where they would suffer from the effects of exposure. One witness to Benjamin's plight would later tell of hearing her repeated distress calls in the night. Another witness described her as emaciated and despondent, but perhaps most of all—lonely.

Starving and cold, Benjamin, the last thylacine, died alone in 1936 as a result of neglect by her caretakers, 59 days after the Tasmanian government declared her species nationally protected.

III. The Chamber

"But let us descend now unto greater sorrow
Already sinks each star that was ascending
When I set out, and loitering is forbidden."

-Dante Alighieri
(Inferno)

24
The Actions of Others

Whenever I think about where my life began, where it *really* began, it always seems to stem back to that twisted assembly behind the house, with its red metallic walls and flat roof made out of junkyard tin. The path to where I am now harks back to what was encountered, revealed and ultimately unleashed from within. It was there I first learned what death really is, it was there I grasped the enormity of its permanence, and I can't help but think perhaps it could have all been avoided had I not engaged on the path towards discovery. But I know now, deep down inside I know, that the horror to ensue truly began long before in a chain of events of which I had no part. Well yes, at one point I would have a role to play, sure, but the blood that would flow was in truth catalyzed by the actions, or perhaps inactions, of others. That is, at least, what I tell myself.

25
All Sorts of Bad Things

As a child, I always feared the ramshackle shed in the backyard, at the edge of the woods. When it snowed, my father would climb up and push the snow off so the shed wouldn't collapse, and since it was never warm for long, a great pile of snow surrounded it.

With the perfect angle, I could barely make out the structure behind the brush as I peered through a cloudy window and across the yard. And sometimes late at night, before slumber, I would gaze out through the glass trying to figure out where exactly those sounds were coming from. Sometimes the sounds were of children crying, sometimes of a woman whimpering, but always the sounds were muffled by the void between light and darkness, the chasm separating the world of the living from the world of the dead.

"You hear them sounds back there?" my father would say to me. "Those are the sounds of the unliving, cuz that shed back there is haunted."

"With ghosts?"

"With all sorts of bad things. Dangerous things.

Things you wouldn't believe."

And so I feared the shed and whatever presence dwelled within, yet its mysteries presented a seductive allure. And sometimes my father would catch me behind our house, staring curiously at the shed, pondering temptation. My father, sipping from his cheap bottle of whiskey, would come out of the house or his truck or wherever he might be, glare at me and shout to stay out.

Knowing the consequences of defiance, I obeyed. And yet, like any child, I wondered most about that which I was denied. And I would glance back at the haunted shed wondering, knowing the day would come when temptation proved too strong.

26
Into Darkness

I had to wait until my father was asleep before I began.

We shared a small, one room house, and slept on a bunk bed built from wood my father had cut down off a long dead tree. The room was barely large enough to contain our bed, a small kitchen area, a fireplace, and a dusty table upon which rested the glass tank where Mr. Eedy always slept, coiled behind a black rock and beside crickets he never seemed hungry enough to eat.

Quite often, those days, my father would stumble in at some point after dark and pass out on the floor beside the fireplace. On a rare night in his bed he was a restless sleeper—tossing and turning, sometimes for hours, entrenched in that frustrating twilight—that bleak perdition where consciousness somehow melts away but there is no break through the ramparts of sleep. His demons, I suppose, wouldn't let him fall easily into slumber's embrace—not without some help first from the bottle.

Benjamin

On that particular night, however, he happened to be in his bed, and before long began snoring heavily, the only telltale sign that he would remain dormant for at least some time, and so I began.

I climbed down from the top bunk, sliding down silently as to not awaken my father and slowly as to suffer no splinters from the jagged frame. Once I reached the floor, I stalled for a moment to ensure he remained asleep. I grabbed a box of matches from beside the fireplace, put on my coat, gloves, and boots, for it had been a terrible winter indeed, and left the house.

Once I closed the door, ever so gently behind me, I listened to the sound of my father's snoring which continued unabated. I crossed the clearing, carefully placing each step to reduce the sound of crunching snow. Far in the distance I heard wolves howling. They sounded sad. And hungry.

That was the closest I had ever been to the haunted shed. The wooden door was rugged and stunk of mildew, and was the structure's only face not blocked by a pile of snow taller than me. I lifted my arm to press the door open, and upon making contact I thought I heard a sound behind me. I spun around but saw only light shining off the snow whenever the moon surfaced from behind hurried white vapors.

The door creaked open with little effort. Only residual moonshine crept in through the doorway so it took time for my eyes to acclimate. I waited in the entry, tempted to light a match, but refrained because the light might alert my father. I listened closely for any change in his snoring which continued muffled from far behind.

After some time I could see the inside of the shed a little. It seemed empty, save a workbench along the far wall with an assortment of items upon it. I entered, approached the bench, and found a hammer, a hatchet, a variety of rusty nails and screws and other battered gadgets. The whole time I felt like there was something else in there with me—some dark presence—watching me, studying my every movement, waiting.

What was I thinking, coming here? In the middle of the night no less! While I didn't see any ghosts, they could have appeared at any moment. To make matters worse, despite that I'd be forewarned if he stopped snoring, I was plagued by the vision of my father's moonlit silhouette standing in the doorway, and I wasn't sure which prospect was more frightening—the threat of the living or the threat of the dead.

Enough was enough. I'm getting out of here, I thought. Then, about to depart, I heard coughing from somewhere down below and my heart began to race. Despite the cold I felt drops of sweat balling up on my forehead, for whatever lurked within seemed to have awakened.

As I hastened out of the shed, I tripped over a dirty rug, pulling it up off the floor. When I put the rug back in place, seeking to leave no sign of my trespass, I noticed a panel on the floor unlike the others. I felt around and indeed there was a crevice beside it, just wide enough to put my fingers through. A secret passage, I thought, and my childlike curiosity swelled up inside me. Risking that a phantom might grab my hand, I put two fingers through the opening and lifted the board.

Below the panel was a black abyss. A ladder made of rope, similar to one that might be used in a rescue, but tattered and abused, went down into the hole as far as I could see. Finding what appeared to be a bottomless pit, in what was already known to me as a haunted structure, sent a shiver through my body. I hesitated a moment, wondering if I should abandon further exploration, but again my curiosity overcame my fear and I decided instead to descend into the darkness.

One step down.

A painful coldness flowed past me as the air from the depths was exchanged with that from above.

Two steps down. Three.

I squeezed the ladder, not knowing what horrors dwelt below. The thought of a ghostly hand grasping my ankle kept running through my mind. I squeezed harder.

Four steps down. Five.

What madness was I descending into? Once my head dipped below the ground I was entirely encased within the vertical channel. As I continued into a blackness profounder than anything I had ever seen, I became dizzy.

Six steps down. Seven.

I exhaled and paused, shuddering at what unknowns my boots could touch on the next step. I might hit the next rung, I might hit a pit of snakes, I might hit nothing at all and plummet forever into oblivion.

Eight steps down. Nine.

My foot settled on a hard surface—I had reached the

bottom. I sighed in fleeting relief, until I realized that I no longer heard my father snoring. I didn't know if he had awakened or if I simply couldn't hear him anymore from this far underground. I hoped it was the latter.

The blackness in the chamber was absolute. I put my arms out as far as I could but felt nothing, as before me stood an emptiness of unknown size. The thought of climbing back up crossed my mind, just to check if I could hear my father snoring again once I got closer to the surface. I knew though that if I went up, I might not have the courage to climb back down. So I lit a match, which I justified as harmless since it probably couldn't be seen from the surface, even though I knew in my heart, even back then, that I really just needed some light or I might go mad from terror. Looking back now, it seems it was then, perhaps for the first time, that I feared something more than my father.

Flickering in the match light I saw before me a long corridor, hardly tall enough for even me, with walls etched in frozen mud and rock. I could barely make out a doorway at the end of the corridor. As I tiptoed towards it, my match went out, and I thought I heard whimpering before me. It is a ghost who has finally come to see me off, I thought, and in a panic I tried to light another match but instead dropped the entire box. In the blackness I heard the wooden sticks sprinkle onto the frozen floor, so I dropped to my knees and felt around frantically. The moaning at the end of the corridor became louder, and in the absence of light perhaps seemed to be coming closer. And closer. Hands shaking, I continued to feel along the floor, the cold rock searing my palms right through the gloves. At last I found a match, a pile of them to be exact, but couldn't grasp a single stick due to the bulky fabric covering my hands. After several failed attempts, I finally yanked off one of my gloves and grabbed a match.

To my relief when I struck it, I was still alone. I picked up the rest of the matches and continued down the corridor.

The door at the end of the tunnel was warped and with even slight pressure appeared to bend. At its center was a horizontal bar lock which prevented it from opening. The bar was firm and refused to budge.

With a dying match in one hand I examined the keyhole while again hearing voices moan beyond the threshold. My heart pounded in my chest, my breathing became heavy, and its icy mist began to envelop me. Whatever terrors waited behind the door appeared to be safely locked away, while at any moment my father could awaken and find me gone, his wrath being one I did not want to face. Although still drawn by the secrets of the chamber, I had reached an impasse, for without the key I could proceed no further.

27
The Hunt

The sun had long since risen when I awoke. I peered over the side of my bunk to see if my father was there, but his bed was empty and his crumpled blankets and stained sheets were halfway on the floor. Inside the fireplace were a few dying embers from which wisps of smoke snaked upwards and away.

The house was empty. I sat up, stretched, and looked out the window to see just how well I had covered my snow tracks in the night. From what I could tell, any evidence of my nighttime excursion had been wiped away, either by my own hand or by the wind.

My father barged into the house and slammed the door behind him. He looked around, sniffed the air, rubbed his unkempt black beard between his index finger and thumb, and grabbed a box of shells from the drawer before turning to me.

"Nice to see you back among the living," he said. "I'm going hunting. Don't go nowhere."

Benjamin

We had always subsisted largely on whatever animals my father managed to hunt down in the surrounding woodland. There was nothing he loved more than the single pounding beat of a bullet tearing through the flesh of an animal. In times of surplus, he might even disappear into the woods just to shoot deer for sport. Lacking a refrigerator, the most recent catch would be left out back, somewhere between the house and the shed, where it would rot long before it had been eaten completely. Eventually my father would take the carcasses to some mysterious resting place, and I suspected that somewhere in the woods was a towering pile of death.

This winter, however, had been especially wicked and there was no wildlife to be found. My father repeatedly walked alone into the wilderness and returned empty-handed. He had caught nothing for so long that we had resorted to living on stale bread, canned beans and dried fruit that he would bring back from some place he called "the old man's store" many miles down the road. I'm not sure where he got the money to buy this food—I know sometimes he'd chop down trees and sell them for firewood and there might be other times he'd be gone for days at a time, leaving me at home to fend for myself. Maybe he was out doing odd jobs that popped up from time to time, I really don't know.

As I rose from bed I thought about the night before—the fear, the suspense, the mystery. I thought about the shed, virtually empty. I thought about the secret panel on the floor, hidden under a rug. I thought about the ladder descending into the blackness and the frozen, cramped corridor below. But mostly, I thought about the door and what might lie beyond. Who had put it there? Who had locked it? Was my father aware of this underground chamber? Should I tell him? If he did know, was it he who locked away the horrors to protect the world from their fury?

Asking my father about the door would require admitting that I had entered the forbidden shed, so as I watched him walk out to his pickup truck, I realized the only way to solve the enigma was to find the key and explore the chamber myself.

As always, it took my father several tries to start the pickup. The truck was old, with wires hanging from the bottom and scraps of rusty metal falling off its fenders. He'd often have to open the hood and mess around with the engine or the oil or whatever just to get it going. Sometimes even that didn't work and his face would get red and he'd start kicking it and calling it names, and I would run and hide. This time, however, he was able to get the old beater going just by revving it a few times, so I was relieved.

When the truck disappeared beyond the hills, I began searching for the key. First I rummaged through the kitchen drawers, searching under papers, under cutlery, some drawers so packed with trash they barely opened. I searched in the cupboards, under the table, beneath the rug and in the fireplace. I searched under the mattresses, under the blankets, under the many empty bottles lining the cabinet tops. I even searched Mr. Eedy's tank, who still hadn't eaten any of his crickets. Outside, I searched beneath every rock, around the perimeter of the house, even in the shed. But nowhere was the key to be found. Given the thoroughness of my exploration, I was convinced that the key either no longer existed or it was on my father's person.

That night, my father returned empty-handed after yet another failed hunt. Reeking of whiskey, he shoved his way through the door in a burst of swirling snow, careening off the doorpost and slamming the door behind him in a single, bumbling motion. I had seen him in this condition before, more times than I care to admit, and I knew it was best to not engage him at all. I watched in silence by the fireplace as he stumbled through our home, mumbling indignantly at himself, knocking things over in his stupor. When he would glance in my direction, he'd look right through me—almost as if I didn't exist at all.

Although this wasn't an unprecedented sight by any means, I found it a bit more unnerving than usual because of the way he gripped his rifle the entire time. Normally he'd stand it up by the door after entering—a sensible thing to do since there was no use for it indoors. This time, however, he clenched the weapon, and after fumbling around a while, stopped in his tracks and aimed it at Mr. Eedy's tank. My instinct was to jump up and scream for him to stop, but I knew all too well that the worst thing I could do was interrupt him and have him redirect his rage towards me. On the verge of tears thinking he was about to blast my poor snake through the glass, I could do nothing but watch, hope, and shield myself in the event the shards exploded everywhere. My father then rotated slowly, the butt of his rifle firmly in the pocket of his shoulder, pointing the firearm at all four walls in succession. After a full rotation, he ended right where he began—his weapon aimed at a defenseless, captive creature that was oblivious to the violence about to befall it. My father stared at it through the rifle's sight for what felt like an eternity before lowering the weapon and flinging it, still cocked and loaded, into the kitchen. It crashed onto the counter, knocking several dirty old cups onto the floor. He stood there for a moment, and after taking a deep breath, tossed his keychain onto the table before throwing himself on the floor beside the fireplace.

I had built the fire myself, and I fed it a few more logs to keep it burning.

I watched my father for quite some time that evening, and once he began snoring heavily I again knew he was completely out. I looked at the keychain he had tossed onto the table and it had two keys: one for the house and one for the truck. Although the chamber key wasn't there, this brought up another possibility—it was hidden in the pickup. I looked down at my comatose father, and after witnessing his haphazard, menacing tour through our home, had to think twice about what I was about to do. But I was just a child, and had already come so far without fully appreciating the danger I would soon foment, so I put on my coat and boots, grabbed the keys, and tiptoed out of the house.

I crossed the yard through the snow and scoured the rickety vehicle. I searched through the glove box and under the seats. I searched in the corroded wheel wells, in the trunk, and under the floor mats. I even looked under the hood, which I knew how to open from seeing my father mess around in there so many times. The key was nowhere.

Discouraged, I returned to the house, where my father remained passed out beside the fireplace. I looked down at him and saw a bulge in his breast pocket that I had somehow missed before. *That* is the key, I thought, and as I reached slowly towards him, hands inches from his chest, he suddenly awoke and grabbed my wrist. He stared at me from below with wide open, bloodshot eyes, mouth agape and drool trickling from his lips, his forehead creased and cheeks red.

"You… tried… tired… tirers…," he mumbled while drifting back into his drunken slumber. As his hand loosened from my wrist, white marks emerged from where his fingers had gripped, and blood had been drawn beneath crescent hollows.

28
The World is a Dark Place

At sunrise, my father awoke in a hot sweat. Since the kitchen sink was, as always, filled with dirty dishes, he ran out of the house with one hand over his mouth, leaving me to close the door behind him to stop the cold air from pouring in. Eventually he returned, hands and face flush from the cold, his flannel shirt dirty and torn, and sat down across the table from me. I waited for him to say something, anything, but he just stared at me breathing deliberate breaths, almost as if he couldn't get it right without concentrating. After he wiped the vomit from his lips, I was going to ask him about the prior evening just to see if he had any recollection, but then thought better of it. If he remembered, he'd make it clear soon enough.

"Daddy," I began, breaking the silence, "why do we keep the shed if it's haunted?"

My father looked to the side, wiped his forehead, and took a few breaths before turning back to me. I couldn't tell if he was actually looking at me or just glaring in my direction.

"Daddy?" I continued, not sure if he was trying to make some sort of point with his stare.

"Just because," he finally said.

"But why don't we tear it down?"

"I told you there are ghosts in there."

"But won't it get rid of the ghosts if they ain't got nowhere to live?"

"If we tear it down, the ghosts'll be set free."

"What's wrong with that?"

"They're dangerous—even to you, as you should know."

"I don't understand, Daddy."

"Ghosts are trapped between life and death."

"Like trees that are dead but still standing?"

"No. Most of the trees that look dead are just sleeping."

"Until spring?"

"Yeah."

"But when a *person* is dead where do they go?"

"They don't go nowhere."

"You mean like to the place where you put a deer if it's dead too long?"

"No. I mean they don't go nowhere. Like the world turns black around them. When you die, boy, your world ends, the lights go out. Maybe the world keeps on goin' without you, but it ain't your world no more."

"Why do we die?"

"Because your birth is a death sentence."

"What does that mean?"

"It means that everyone dies sooner or later. People. Animals. Sometimes we kill the animals, sometimes they kill each other. Sometimes people even kill people. It can be quick, other times it'll drag on forever."

"But if you've been good you won't feel no pain right?"

"It don't matter what you done. Sooner or later everyone suffers."

"That sounds scary."

"The world is a dark place, boy."

The conversation was heading in a direction that was, at the time, far too heavy for my innocent ears. So I changed the topic back to ghosts, which was, in my naïve worldview, much simpler. "Soooo… ghosts are people who died but are still part of the world?"

"Sometimes the ghosts have to stay cuz in life they did something bad. Real bad. And they ain't allowed to go to the other side until they make things right."

"What bad things did the ghosts in the shed do?"

"Nothing. I dunno," he replied while turning away and peering into the fireplace. A piece of wood snapped and a spark was ejected from the hearth. "But they obviously did something or they wouldn't be there" he resumed, staring into the flames.

"You said Mommy died when I was born, right?"

"Yep."

"Did the lights go out for her too?"

My father turned towards Mr. Eedy's tank and rubbed his fingers up and down the glass. He tapped the glass twice, then once more, then began rubbing it again before turning back to me.

"You shut the fuck up, boy. We don't talk about your mother," he said, each staccato word cleanly articulated and disconnected from the last.

29
The Wire

The chamber door beckoned. I now had the key, having stolen it off my father who had once again, following a bottle of booze, forsaken consciousness beside the fireplace. He had lain on his back with his hands crossed over his chest, and when I had reached towards his breast pocket, he grunted and rolled into the fetal position. But I had been determined to take the key, and again reached in and succeeded on the second try.

I grabbed a flashlight this time in lieu of matches. When I opened the front door, frigid air poured into the house with a wolf-like howl, and for a moment I thought my father may have awakened. But he remained asleep, and I continued on across the yard, into the shed, and down the ladder.

The key was shiny and new, much like the bar lock, in contrast to the flimsy, battered door guarding the world from the undead. With a flashlight in one hand, I slid the key into the keyhole, and before turning it, again heard a sound from beyond the threshold. It seemed almost like a frightened weeping, as if whatever was on the other side feared the unknown entity without more than I feared the unknown entity within. I paused for a moment and remembered the day I had caught Mr. Eedy in the backyard. Don't worry boy, that snake is more afraid of you than you are of him, my father had told me.

I turned the key and lifted the bar lock. Trembling, I slowly pulled open the door. The smells of feces, urine and filth were overwhelming and when I lowered the light beam into the chamber, white mice scattered towards the walls.

The chamber was about five feet high and barely wider. Like the tunnel, its walls were made of rock and frozen mud, and its frigid interior was about as unfit for human habitation as one could imagine. Yet a humanlike figure was curled on the floor with their arms wrapped around a metal pole in the center of the chamber, their wrists pressed together by rusty shackles. Their hair was frayed and stuck out sideways in crooked shocks over the collar of an oversized coat, and when the prisoner looked up at me with her mournful brown eyes, I saw at once she was a woman. Her skin was translucent and pale, with grime plastered on her cheeks and tortured sores on her neck. Around the back of her head and between her lips was a triangular copper wire. Shiny metallic tape covered her mouth and several threadbare blankets covered her body.

I was frozen. I had expected the chamber to contain

something supernatural, something not of this world, not the human prisoner before me. Then I thought perhaps this was an illusion, an apparition of some hideous event that had happened long ago, and I began to tremble again. I started to retreat, ready to flee back to the house in horror, when suddenly the prisoner made a sound. Although her beckoning was incoherent beneath her gag, I saw she spoke directly to me, as she gazed at me from below.

I squeezed my eyes shut, as if doing so would make this all go away, but I couldn't even pretend since I could still hear her. What was she trying to say? She was obviously trying to communicate something to me, and I just had to know what it was. So I held my breath and removed the tape from her mouth. I can't imagine how it must have felt as I slowly peeled it off her, but given the looks of things this was probably nothing compared to the pain she'd already suffered. After I took off the tape, the prisoner began to cough, face down into the black stripes of her blanket, and it took a while for her to catch her breath. Finally she gathered herself and looked up at me.

"Peez...take coat hanga out...," she begged, her voice brittle and frail.

I was pretty sure she was talking about the metal wire in her mouth. The wire had been twisted together behind her head, so I unwound it and took it off of her. Once I had removed it, she slunk down into the blanket and began to sob. I put my hand on her shoulder and she looked up at me again.

"Child... is that you?" she asked through thin,

cracked lips.

"Um... I guess?"

"But he always told me you perished."

"I don't know what that means," I said while placing the tangled wire onto the floor.

The woman stared blankly at the wire for a moment, and then turned back to me after a long, single blink. "Are you real?" she asked with her eyes darting back and forth.

"I'm real."

"You... you seem different than the others. Like the one who comes in the night."

"I don't know what you're talking about."

The woman buried her face into the blanket and then looked back up at me. "I need food. Water. He hasn't brought me anything in days. Please help me."

"We don't have no food. We finished the last of the bread today. And Daddy hasn't brought home a kill for weeks."

"Water...?"

I nodded. "Yeah, but I can't bring it to you tonight. I need to get back before Daddy wakes up and finds me gone."

"Boy, you have to help me," said the woman while lifting her shackled wrists towards me.

"I will. I'll bring you some water—I just can't do it right now."

"You can't just leave me here."

As I gazed into her filmy eyes, I thought about what my father had said earlier that day. The ghosts in the shed had to stay locked away because in life they had done something bad. Was she a real person or was she some sort of specter, stuck between life and death? If she was a ghost, what had she done to condemn herself to this eternal limbo? Was this some sort of trick maybe? Some sort of trap? By letting her free what kind of evil would I be unleashing upon the world?

For a moment I thought about my father passed out beside the fireplace. Although unlikely, he could be awake right now, wondering where I am, walking around the house or the yard looking for me and calling my name. Between the mystery of the woman and the threat of my father, I was so overcome with feelings and fears that even at that age I knew I had to get out of there; I just couldn't get it together. I guess, you could say, I was close to panicking.

"Not tonight. I need to get back," I responded. I put the wire and tape back on her, thinking that she would resist, but she didn't. As I closed the door behind me, I saw a mouse scurry along a wall. "Do they keep you company?" I asked.

The woman shrugged.

I closed the door and climbed out of the chamber, carefully putting the floor panel and rug back into place and then covering my tracks in the snow. I entered the house as quietly as possible so I wouldn't disturb my father. Luckily, he remained asleep beside the fireplace, his snores reverberating throughout our home.

There was one more thing I had to do—somehow get the chamber key back into my father's pocket so my nighttime adventures would remain undiscovered. This

Benjamin

shouldn't have been a big deal, except he was now lying flat on his stomach, making his breast pocket inaccessible. With no other options, I put the key on the ground beside him, hoping he'd believe it had fallen out.

30
The Key

My father was drinking a half empty bottle of whiskey while a second, full bottle sat on the table in front of him. As he stared at Mr. Eedy, and Mr. Eedy stared back, one of the few remaining live crickets jumped into the glass with a plink. I sat down across the table, and after a period of silence leaned in towards the tank, puzzled at the uneaten cricket corpses piled up in the corner.

"Mr. Eedy hasn't eaten in a long time."

My father shrugged. "Maybe he ain't hungry."

"A snake's gotta eat sometime though."

"Yep."

"So why don't he eat the crickets?"

"I dunno."

"Maybe he feels bad about it?"

"Maybe."

"Can't he tell they just die anyway?"

"He's just a snake, boy."

Benjamin

Not that my father was ever all that talkative, but his demeanor this morning made me feel like something was amiss. I looked around, hoping to uncover a clue as to what was really going on. I saw the fireplace, Mr. Eedy's tank, the bottle of whiskey and finally I looked down at the table where I noticed the chamber key sitting right out in the open between us. I tried to not allow my eyes to linger, and when I looked away from the key and back at my father, his eyes stared into my own like barrels of a gun.

"So how you been?" he said, leaning in towards me with an eyebrow raised.

"I'm... good I guess."

"You been hungry?"

"Yeah, but it don't look like there's any game out there to be had."

"No, it sure don't."

"Where have all the animals gone?"

"Hell if I know."

"Will they ever come back?"

"I dunno. Maybe one day. Who knows."

"What are we gonna do for food then? Maybe you need to go back down to the old man's store?"

"Yeah, maybe."

Despite my every intention, I kept eyeing the key, wondering if my father had put it there as a patent signal that he knew more than he said. Every time I looked, I could tell he caught my gaze, so I turned towards the fireplace, where a few dying embers crackled.

"You remember me coming in last night?"

"Yeah," I replied, still looking into the flames.

"What were you doing when I got back?"

"I was in bed."

"Asleep?"

"No, not yet."

"Tell me about when I came in," he said while gulping from the bottle.

Something about this wasn't normal; never before had my father asked me to describe his drunken escapades. I had to make sure to not say anything that could possibly give away or even hint at my nighttime capers. I had to play it innocent; I had to play it clean. I had to make eye contact with him when I spoke and stop gazing into the fire.

"You looked really tired. Then you went to sleep next to the fireplace," I replied, returning my eyes to him.

"What time was it?"

"I don't know, it was pretty late though."

"Did I get up at all?"

"No."

"Was I rolling around a lot?"

"Some."

"Snoring?"

"Yeah."

"A lot?"

"Not any more than usual."

"And what you do after I fell asleep?"

"I went back to bed."

"*Straight* back to bed?"

"Yeah, Daddy. I went straight back to bed."

Benjamin

Now I was really getting worried. He had to suspect some sort of mischievousness on my part, otherwise why the inquisition? If only he hadn't been lying on his stomach when I came back the night before! I would have been able to put the key back in his pocket and he wouldn't have suspected a thing. I had to be extra careful here; even the slightest mistake or misspoken answer would give everything away.

"So how'd you sleep?" he continued.

"Okay, I guess."

"*You* get up at all?"

"No, I stayed in bed the whole night."

"What's 'the whole night' mean?"

"You know... like until the morning."

"What'd you do between the time I fell asleep and you went to bed?"

"Nothing, Daddy."

"You sure about that?"

"Yeah Daddy I swear it." As I said this, I peeked at the key, almost like it was some sort of reflex; I just couldn't help myself. I instantly turned away, returning my gaze towards the fireplace like it was some sort of crutch. I had done so well up until then too—looking right at my father as I spoke, answering each question as if I was clueless; as if I believed he really was just interested in our sleeping arrangements. I don't know what made me lose my focus. Maybe I just couldn't keep up the charade forever, maybe I was getting too nervous. Whatever it was, at that point I couldn't hold it in any longer, the key drew my gaze like a lure, and I'm sure I hadn't done myself any favors by looking guilty and turning away so fast.

"You sure you didn't go outside? Like maybe just for a minute or two?"

"I'm sure."

"I thought I heard the door open at one point, you sure that wasn't you?"

"No, I went straight to bed."

"What was it I heard then?"

"I don't know what you heard; I don't think you heard nothing. Maybe it was a dream?"

"It wasn't no dream."

"Then I don't know."

"You remember how we talked about the rules before?"

"Yeah."

"What's the rule about the shed?"

"I'm not allowed in there."

"And why ain't you allowed in there?"

"Cuz it's haunted."

"Tell me the rule again."

"What?"

"Tell me again."

"The rule about the shed?"

"Damnit, boy. Yes, the rule about the shed. What the fuck were we just talking about?"

"I'm not allowed in there. Never."

Silence. As I sat there waiting for the next question, my father wiped the brown spirit off his lips with his sleeve. He then exploded to his feet, knocking over the

Benjamin

chair behind him, and then hurled the bottle of whiskey into the fireplace where it shattered, sending orange embers outwards in a puff of smoke. He grabbed me by the collar, pulled me halfway onto the table, and struck me in the eye with a crack. It felt like I had been hit with a baseball bat.

"You know the rules, boy, you know the rules!" he screamed with veiny eyes inches from my own, his hot, whiskey infused breath flowing over me.

I yelped and squirmed, almost knocking Mr. Eedy's tank onto the floor, and then was dropped. I slid off the table into a heap while salty rivulets streamed down my cheeks.

My father grabbed his rifle and stormed out of the house, leaving me curled up under the table. I felt a wetness on my cheek that I knew had to be more than tears. I touched below my eye and felt a fissure. When I pulled my hand away, my fingertips were covered in blood and the tears streaming into the cut stung like liquid skewers.

31
The Last One on Earth

When I dreamt that night, mountains of ice crumbled and fell into the sea, flooding the coastlands, imprisoning the masses and separating each man from his brother, each child from their mother.

When I dreamt that night, my father raised a rifle in exchange for a coin. As he pointed his weapon into the desolation, I felt he and I were perhaps two faces of that coin, and that some remote drifter may, one day, come and free me.

When I dreamt that night, I was imprisoned behind bars that appeared like stripes before the twilight. I feigned slumber as my father gazed upon me from without.

When I dreamt that night, I stepped into my father's footprints as to leave no sign of my own. Standing tall above the chamber, I watched him climb underground, leaving a pale cone of light as evidence of his descent. In the chamber below he hollered that she would make it fucking right and in turn she cried.

And screamed.

When, as a child, I dreamt that night, I was the last one on earth.

32
Mr. Eedy

You shouldn't drive in this condition, I thought, as my father stumbled into his truck. I'm going hunting, he slurred, but I doubted he would succeed given both his condition and the dearth of game plaguing us all winter. He had been out there messing with the crippled pickup all morning, trying to get it to start, and I stayed as far away as I could as he hollered and beat on the hood. Finally he succeeded, and I wondered just how many rides it had left in it.

My throbbing eye had swollen into a fat red knob. After my father left I looked at my reflection in the window and saw that the gash under my eye was a couple inches long and gaped open the width of my pinky. The blood had stopped dripping yet the cut itself was full of a syrupy gunk when I touched it. I looked at my hand to find that the red had been mixed with a thick yellow pus. I peered back into my reflection, and blurred in the distance, was the shed.

Benjamin

My father either hadn't noticed or didn't care about the condition of my face, but his stupor afforded one advantage—he had left the chamber key atop the table once more, and I wondered if he had ever carelessly left it out in the past without me noticing.

You might ask yourself why, after my father's terrorizing interrogation, I didn't just do as I was told and stay away from the shed. But I had to go back—back down into the chamber. There was, at least, unfinished business—I had told the prisoner I'd bring her some water. And she sure looked like she needed it. She sure looked like she needed a lot of things.

My promise to her wasn't really my motivation to return, though. What drove me was, once again, my curiosity. The more I learned about the chamber, the more I wanted to discover all of its secrets. And the more my father forbade my entry, the more meaningful and worthwhile those secrets seemed to be.

Also, you have to understand, I never really had been exposed to other people. It was just me and my father out there—that's it. Whatever that presence was in the chamber, be she a person or a ghost, she was the closest thing to another human I had ever seen. And if I felt isolated living out there alone with my father, how must she feel, stuck down there all by herself? Maybe she wasn't even a ghost at all; maybe she was just lonely and needed a friend. So after I filled up a bottle of water, I put it, along with Mr. Eedy, into a small burlap sack and then descended into the chamber.

When I lowered the light beam into her cell the

woman turned away, clearly bothered by the light, and I noticed she had a black eye and a blotch on the side of her neck like someone had been clutching it. It made me wonder about my dream the night before. As I stood there pondering this, I caught her looking at my cut.

"What happened to your eye?"

I looked down at the floor and didn't answer.

"Did your Daddy do that?"

I shrugged.

"You better clean out that cut, it already looks infected."

I felt like I was going to cry, but held it in.

"Why did he do this to you?"

"He wanted to remind me to behave, I think."

"Did it work?"

"No," I said, knowing that my presence alone may have answered the question. I stared back at the woman, who adjusted her blankets with her teeth. "Aren't you cold?"

"Very. But you get used to it. I have a warm coat and heavy blankets. And at least there's no wind. But I don't know how many more winters I'll last."

"I'd bring you another blanket but I don't think we have any extras."

"It's okay, I'll manage. But hey—you didn't happen to bring me any water like we talked about last time?"

"I did, actually." I reached into the sack and handed her the water. She guzzled the entire bottle. "Wow—you were thirsty."

"I was, thank you."

Benjamin

"I can probably bring you more later; I just gotta wait until the next time my Daddy goes out. I'm not supposed to be down here."

"Is that what happened to your eye?"

"What do you mean?"

"Did he do that to your eye because you came down here last time?"

"I think so."

"And yet you came down here again?"

"Yeah."

"Why?"

"Cuz I told you I'd bring you water."

"That wasn't the first time you were down here, was it?"

"No."

"One time you were out in the tunnel but stopped at the door. That was you, wasn't it?"

"Yeah, that was me."

"You stop because you were scared or because you didn't have the key?"

"Well I was a little scared, I guess—but I was already down here. I went back up because I didn't have the key."

"How'd you finally get it?"

"I took it off my Daddy while he was sleeping."

"He asleep now?"

"No, he went out hunting."

"Do you know when he's coming back?"

"No. Sometimes he comes back quick, other times he'll be gone awhile." The woman nodded with a look of concern and we both stared at one another in silence, both perhaps recognizing the danger of my father finding us down there together. I didn't want to think about it so I changed the subject. "How long have you been here?" I finally asked.

"I don't know. I can't tell day or night. They blend into each other like a big long now."

"Because it's always dark down here?"

"Yeah. When you first come to a place like this, you don't realize how long it's going to be for. It seems… I dunno… temporary."

"Like not for always?"

"Yes. At first, you keep thinking that at any moment you'll be set free. You hold on, I guess, to your old life. You know… to the way things were. But as time passes and nothing changes you surrender to a new reality."

"You give up?"

"I guess so, yes."

"To what?"

"To a darkness that lasts forever, I suppose."

"But don't you still get hungry sometimes?"

"Yes. I'm hungry right now."

"What do you do for food?"

"Your Daddy brings me food and water, comes to change my buckets. Hasn't done either in some time though."

"He knows you're here?"

"He knows I'm here."

"Are you lonely?"

"Not while you're here."

"Look," I said while putting down the burlap sack. "I

brought you company." I lifted the sack and Mr. Eedy thumped onto the rocky floor. "This is Mr. Eedy."

The woman looked at the snake. "I don't know, I think Mr. Eedy might actually be a girl."

"How do you know?"

"Hard to tell. But sometimes the tail gives it away."

"Oh."

"Anyway, thank you, but I don't know if I want a snake loose down here with me."

"He'll help with the mice though."

"That's okay. They keep me company, I guess."

I put Mr. Eedy back into the sack. "You're not a ghost, are you?"

"What do you think?"

"I dunno. I'm not sure."

"Well no, I'm not a ghost."

"Ghosts are people that are trapped between the world of the living and the world of the dead, that's what Daddy says."

"Well then maybe I'm a ghost."

"What did you do so that you can't go to the other side?"

"I guess I must have done something bad. Or at least something your Daddy thinks was bad," she said, eyeing the wire that had been fastened around her head.

"Last time you said I'm not like the others. Did you mean like my Dad?"

"No, there are others down here. I don't see them but I can hear them."

"Other ghosts?"

Her eyes returned to me. "Kid, I'm not a ghost."

"But you just said you are."

"I know I said that. I was kidding. Sort of."

"Then what do you hear?"

"I don't know. But there's something else."

"Is it here now?"

"No."

"What does it say?"

"It tells me…I dunno… things."

"Who is it?"

"The nameless one."

"Who?"

"She comes back to say the words muted before her first breath."

"Okay now I'm really confused."

She sighed. "That is how he punishes me, you see. He chains me in the abyss to be tormented by her."

This conversation was starting to spook me out. I began to think, ghost or not, this woman might be surrounded by them. Either that or she was losing her grip on sanity. As lucid as she had been throughout this conversation, there was something else going on. Maybe her time trapped in the chamber had taken a toll on her mind. "You look like you feel pretty bad for whatever it is you did. Maybe he can let you go now."

"Your Daddy won't let me go until I make good on what I've done. He comes down here sometimes to help me make it right. But I just don't know if I can anymore."

"I don't know what that means."

"You shouldn't. You're too young to know."

Benjamin

"Did he try to help you make it right last night?"

The woman didn't answer; she instead stared past me and down the corridor while her mouth trembled and she held back tears. "You look like a good boy," she said. "I always knew you would've been. Maybe you can help me break these chains."

"I don't know. Daddy would be mad."

"But you said I look like I feel bad enough for what I've done. How about you help a nice lady?"

I wanted to help her but carried too much fear of my father's rage. "I have to go. I don't know when my Daddy's gonna be back. He went out hunting."

"It's okay. I know you don't want both eyes looking like that. But think about what I said. I'm sorry for what I've done. You can see I'm sorry, you said it yourself. So next time you come down here, maybe you'll help me leave. That's what a good boy would do."

"I'll think about it," I said, before hearing a faraway gunshot from somewhere up above. My father must have bagged a deer and would be bringing it home soon, I thought. "I gotta go," I said again, before putting the gags back on her and climbing out of the chamber.

When I reached the yard, I looked out into the forest, hoping that spring might one day come. Then I thought again about the captive woman, and set Mr. Eedy on the ground, letting her free forever.

33
Trying to Get Paid

My father didn't bring home a kill that day, but I was awakened the next by more gunshots. My head was pounding as I rose from bed and the cut under my eye itched dreadfully. I tried to scratch it but when I touched my face it burned as if scalded by hot coals. The wound was still wet and the discharge had turned a yellowish green.

Again I heard a boom cry out, so I walked out of the house to see what all the noise was about. My father stood outside in the grey fog, wearing nothing but boxers and boots, his rifle aimed at a tree. His coat lay on the snow beside him, a full bottle of whiskey stood at his feet, and several empty beer cans littered the ground around him. Repeated gusts turned falling snow into clouds and puffs that swirled around the yard, and whatever landed on him would quickly melt and stream down his bare back. I thought perhaps he mumbled something about stripes, but it was hard to tell.

Benjamin

"Hey Dad, what are you doing?"

"Trying to get paid," he said before cocking his gun, firing at the tree, and taking a violent swig of whiskey.

"Hey Dad..."

My father took the rifle into both hands and held it sideways across his chest. He then turned to me and nodded towards the shed. "All that snow. Them snow piles around the shed. They melted."

I looked over at the shed and the large banks burying the sides of the edifice appeared unchanged. They were perhaps even growing on account of the snowfall. In retrospect the incongruous behavior of the snow he had witnessed was a hallucination, but at the time I didn't understand what was happening to him. His sinister bearing made it obvious though that arguing with him wasn't the wisest path forward, so I shrugged my shoulders as if I agreed.

As we locked eyes, he nodded—assuming, I guess, that I saw what he saw. He raised an eyebrow at me before cocking his weapon and shooting again at the tree, whose impact site was now scarred with a distorted cleft.

"Hey Daddy..."

He didn't even bother to look at me or acknowledge in any way that I had spoken. Instead, he walked up to the tree, looked closely at the gash in the trunk, and put his finger into the opening. He shook his head and frowned as if dissatisfied.

"Daddy, my face hurts. And I don't feel good."

He glanced at me and then walked over to the whiskey bottle and chugged. He belched and put the bottle back down. "Then don't think about it," he finally said.

"Daddy I think we need to do something about my face."

Silence.

"It hurts and there's this green stuff coming out of it."

My father rolled his eyes and took another swig of whiskey. Then he loaded the rifle and shot the tree again. "How many times you reckon I gotta shoot it before it falls?" he asked to no one in particular.

"I don't know? A lot? Daddy, my face really hurts…"

"That's all I'll be hearing about your face!" he snapped.

I didn't know what to say. I watched him shoot the tree yet again. Clearly he wasn't concerned about my infection, and I figured I'd better drop the subject or who knows, he might just turn his rifle on me. So I changed the topic to hunting since I hadn't eaten in days; maybe all I needed was a little food in my system to help me start getting better.

"Hey I thought I heard a gunshot out in the woods yesterday. Was that you?"

Silence.

"Did you get a deer?"

Another shot at the tree, another sip of whiskey.

"Dad, we need food. I'm hungry. Did you get any deer?"

Silence.

"Ok so was it an elk then? A moose? A rabbit? That gunshot was you right?"

Benjamin

Silence.

"Daddy, you're scaring me."

My father cocked his weapon, admired the black alloy of the barrel, and rubbed it along his temple before pointing it upwards and away. Then he paused, aimed again at the tree, but without firing pulled it back and rested the muzzle on the ground. He turned to me and stared for a long, uncomfortable moment, and I was afraid to speak.

"What happened to Mr. Eedy?" he finally asked, tapping the tip of the rifle on the snow.

For a moment I thought I'd declare innocence, perhaps feign devastation at the loss of my friend, but then thought better of it. My father would see right through the lie.

"I... I let her go," I confessed.

"Her?"

"I let *it* go."

"Why the fuck you do that?"

"I... I thought maybe it didn't want to be in a cage anymore."

My father looked back at the shed and just kept staring at it. He seemed to want to approach it, and I thought perhaps a look of sadness may have come over him. But then he turned back to me, scowled, grabbed his coat and climbed into his truck without saying another word.

The engine made a sad groaning sound but wouldn't start. My father tried again and failed. As he tinkered under the hood, I somehow felt that the truck represented my only way out of what was becoming a hellish reality, and any chance of escape was quickly fading with the truck in its death throes. Finally, however, he got it to start, and as he drove away, wide, colorless tire tracks scarred the fresh snow and a black cloud of exhaust wafted over me.

34
Wide, Colorless Tire Tracks

The sun had set and risen with no sign of my father's return. The whole side of my face burned, most of my body now ached, and on top of it all I was dreadfully hungry.

In spite of my worsening condition, I was obsessed with the woman in the chamber. I thought about her anguish, locked away in a hole, grimy and scarred, frail from lack of food, and light, and clean air. As I pondered her and her appearance, her voice and her scent, I knew she could be no apparition. She was no charade of the unliving, no deception set forth to fool a child into unleashing the undead. No—*that* she could not be. That was just a story; a tale dreamt up by my father to keep me from finding out what was actually going on in there, a lie meant only to control me and keep her locked away forever. That woman was his prisoner—and he her tormentor. Yet she was alive—a living, breathing being that must be set free, but the door was locked and its key unfound.

As naïve as I might have been, I was quickly learning that what my father had said was true. The world was a dark place indeed, and few things could be as dark as what went on in the chamber. And so it was that I saw the world, for the first time, for what it truly was. I saw the darkness imbued in the body of all things. I saw everywhere the folly of man. And yet, despite all this, little did I foresee the magnitude of what was to come. Little did I predict that the final consummation of such a hateful passage would soon take place with *me* in the chamber—a showdown that would ultimately end my life as I knew it and send me on that bleak journey into the everlasting white desolation of the world beyond.

I really hadn't thought things through before I began. Not having the key to the chamber would, as it turned out, be the least of my problems once I got down there. But I was determined—this woman would be set free by my hand, and I was going to do it now while my father was gone. When else could I have done it, in the middle of the night when he might awaken? True, he could have returned at any moment and caught me down there, but I somehow thought I'd be able to get away with it. So, despite having no plan, no key, an empty stomach, and a rapidly deteriorating physical state, I grabbed my coat, gloves, and boots, and climbed down into the chamber.

"Lady, are you in there?"

The woman grunted, her voice muffled by the gags.

"I'm gonna to set you free."

The woman again made a sound, this time ending in a higher pitch that sounded like surprise.

Benjamin

I nodded, as if she could see through the door. "But you need to take me with you. I don't feel good. And my Daddy's acting crazy. Even worse than normal. I dunno what he'll do when he finds out I let you go."

The woman made a sound that I interpreted as consent.

"But I don't have the key anymore. Daddy must have taken it, and I dunno where he is."

The woman began thumping on the door with her feet, which startled me at first, but I quickly realized she was suggesting that I break down the door. I knew that although the door was flimsy, I didn't have the strength to break it down empty-handed. However, we would probably be able to crawl under the bar lock without much trouble, so all I had to do was figure out a way past the door. Then I remembered the hatchet I had seen in the shed.

"Hold on a sec," I said, before returning to the chamber door. "See if you can get behind the pole. I'm gonna try to break down the door. I don't wanna hurt you."

After some shuffling, the woman clanged her shackles on the pole to signal she was ready.

I swung the hatchet, and the first time it thwacked against the wood, barely making a dent. But the second time, the head went straight through the door, almost causing me to drop the hatchet on the other side.

"Oh no—are you okay?" I asked, concerned that I might have hit her with the blade.

She made a sound to signal that she was okay.

I gripped the handle and tried to yank the hatchet back, but I couldn't muscle it through the wood, so I aligned the blade with the hole I had made and pulled it out. It only took a few more swings to really fracture the door, and once an adequate gap had opened, I pulled off a piece of rotten wood large enough for me to enter the chamber. I slipped through the crack and placed the flashlight on the floor beside the woman, who had to scoot over to make room for me.

"What about the shackles?" I asked while ungagging her.

"The metal's rusted. Maybe you can break it with the hatchet," she said while pulling her hands towards her so that the chain stretched firmly against the pole. She kicked the striped blanket away and braced herself. "Okay I'm ready. Do it."

We were in very close quarters, especially with the chamber door closed. Fearing an errant swing would injure her, I brought the hatchet down in a short arc. The clang of steel against steel reverberated throughout the chamber and sent the woman cringing to the ground.

We examined the chain. No change. I tried again. Still nothing.

"I can't do it. I ain't strong enough."

"Try again!"

I swung a third time, now starting with the blade over my head, having gained some confidence in my aim. The rusty chain jangled but remained unbroken. Then I swung a fourth time. Then a fifth. Not a crack, not a dent. Nothing.

Benjamin

"I just ain't strong enough, maybe you wanna try?" I stupidly suggested.

"I won't be able to get the right angle since I'm chained in."

"But there's gotta be another way."

"Alright, plan B. Look up here. You see these?" She motioned towards where the pole met the ceiling. The pole ended in a flat steel mount that had been screwed into the rock. She then motioned towards the other end of the pole which was affixed to the floor in the exact same fashion—four screws, one at each corner of the mount. "If we can remove the screws from one of the ends, we might be able to tilt the pole so that we can slip the chain either over or under it."

"But how do we get them out?"

"Hand me the flashlight." I handed it to her. She pointed it at the floor and then at the ceiling, examining the screws, and shook her head. "I don't know if it'll work. The screws are a mess; they're all rusty and stripped. They're also probably very deep in the rock. I don't know if we'll be able to get them out."

"What else can we try?"

"I don't know...I guess we can try them anyway. You see how the screw has a sort of star shape in it?"

"Yeah," I said, even though the screw didn't really have a star shape in it anymore. It looked more like a circle with vestigial prongs.

"Go up and see if you can find a screwdriver with a matching tip."

"Okay but I gotta be quick. I don't know when my

Daddy's coming back."

"So go!"

I climbed up into the shed but before looking for any tools I peeked out into the yard. Phew—no sign of my father's truck. I went back into the shed and over to the workbench, where there were several screwdrivers, one which seemed to be the right size. I grabbed it and returned to the chamber.

The woman looked at what I had brought. "Yeah this is the right kind. I still don't know if it'll work with the condition of the screws and all. One way to find out though—give it a try." She pointed the flashlight at the floor while I tried to unscrew the mount.

"It ain't working! The screw won't turn."

"Try a different one."

I tried a another screw. Then a third. Then a fourth. The screwdriver just scraped along the tip and wouldn't grip the rusty metal. It was too corroded, too bare.

"I can't get it to grab."

"Try the ceiling."

I tried to loosen one of the screws in the ceiling but it was too high; I couldn't get the leverage.

"Here, let me try," she said. I traded her the screwdriver for the flashlight. She awkwardly maneuvered around the pole, trying to loosen each of the screws, but none turned even the slightest bit.

"Fuck!" she screamed, slamming the screwdriver into the pole. She then slunk to the ground and pulled the striped blanket back onto her. "I just don't know what else to do."

Benjamin

"Maybe we should try a different screwdriver? There were a whole bunch of them up there."

"It's not the screwdriver. The screws themselves are just too stripped."

"There's gotta be something else we can try."

"I can't think of any other way to undo this—not without the key to the cuffs. I don't suppose you know where it is, do you?"

I hadn't thought of that. "Hmmm... I don't know. I've looked everywhere. It took me forever just to find the key to the chamber door."

"Do you think your father might have hidden it somewhere?"

"I can't think of where it would be. I really looked everywhere. Inside, outside, in his truck, even in his pockets. I don't think there are any other keys."

"I wouldn't put it past him to have thrown it away."

"Well he had the key to the door..."

"Yeah but that's different, he needs it to let himself in. The only reason to keep the key to the cuffs is if he planned on one day letting me go."

"So what do we do?"

"I really don't know, I can't think of anything else..."

"No other way?"

"Is there someone you can call for help?"

"Our phone don't work, and no one ever comes around. It's not like we have neighbors."

"And you have no idea when your father's coming home?"

"No..."

When she asked about my father, I imagined his mud covered boots climbing down the ladder behind me, and my heart started pounding. He had left in such haste the day before—and as usual I had no idea where he had gone or when he would return. Or if, for that matter, he would return at all. He had been acting so crazy too—I couldn't bear to think what he might do if he caught me down here in the chamber. If he showed up now, I was literally down in a hole with nowhere to hide or flee, almost like one of Mr. Eedy's crickets. Only the crickets had mostly just waited out their sentences in his tank, scarcely noticed by their would-be executioner, eventually perishing when their time had come. Was that to be my fate, down here in the chamber? Was my destiny to be chained underground, slowly withering into the void until I myself became one with the blackness?

Even if my father came home and found me in the house, minding my own business, his behavior would have been unpredictable. It wasn't like I would have found asylum by abandoning the woman and returning to the surface, acting as if it was business as usual when my father returned. I knew that I, like she, one way or another needed to escape this madness. And we had to do it now. And yet, I couldn't make it out there on my own, I was just too young—I needed an adult. I needed some sort of guidance to navigate the outside world. I needed her. But here she was, hopelessly jailed in this subterranean nightmare. The irony of needing help from the person I came to save was not lost on me.

"Come on there has to be some way to do this…

think!" I finally cried out.

The woman shook her head while tilting her chin towards the ground. "I don't know if I can go through with it..."

"Go through with what?"

"There is, I guess, one other way."

"Okay?"

"Let me see the hatchet again."

I showed her.

"It's surprisingly sharp isn't it?"

"I guess so."

"Pull up my sleeve."

I pulled the sleeve of her coat up past her elbow.

The woman looked at her arm. "My wrists are pretty thin aren't they?"

"Yeah."

The woman stared at her wrists. She was clearly thinking of something, so I gave her time to ponder whatever she was considering.

"I need to get out of here today," she said. "I have to. I can't wait any longer. I don't know when the next chance will be, or if there will even be another chance at all."

"Okay—but how?"

"Cut off my hand."

"What?!"

"Cut it off."

"No!"

"You don't understand, I am going to die down here. I'm fading, slowly. Every day I slide further and further into the darkness."

"I'm not cutting off your hand!"

"It'll be okay. We just need to be ready to stop the bleeding."

"I'm not cutting off your hand," I said again, this time with more resolve.

"This is the only way. The chains won't break; that much is clear. My wrists are thin though, my bones unhealthy. You should be able to cut right through."

This was a bad idea. I had chopped up firewood before so I knew my strength—and it always took me several chops to break through the wood, no matter how old or dry it was. So, even if I had the strength to cut through her wrist, how many hacks would it take? This was going to get messy.

"I don't know if I can do it."

"Yes you can."

"How are you gonna climb up the ladder with one hand?"

"I'll manage."

"I don't know about this."

"I've been through so much already, I'll make it through. And if not, at least I tried."

I looked at the blade.

"Look," she continued, "our biggest concern here is the blood. There's gonna be a lot of it, and we'll need to stop it right away or I'll bleed out. Tear off a strip of the blanket—just tear it here, along this stripe."

The blanket was in tatters, so I tore off a strip easily.

"You got a fire going up in your house?"

Benjamin

"Yeah."

The woman took a deep breath. "Wrap the strip around my arm here."

I started wrapping it.

"No, you gotta make it tighter. As tight as you can."

I made it tighter. We waited until her forearm began turning red.

"Okay, that'll do. Now there's still going to be a lot of blood, even with this. We're gonna have to stick the stump in the fire to cauterize it."

"I dunno what that means but okay."

"Just help me up the ladder and remember to make sure I stick my hand in the fire once we get up there."

"Okay."

"Alright, are you ready?"

"Ready for what?"

"You're going to cut my hand off."

"No!"

"Yes, we have to."

"I'm not cutting your hand off, forget it!"

"Listen to me," she said, grabbing my arm, "I need to get out—now. We both know it. That's why you're down here risking everything. If we don't escape we're going to have to face your Daddy, who'll know what you did today. There's no way of hiding that hole in the door. We've come too far. This is the only way out—for both of us."

I couldn't believe we were even talking about this, but I did see her logic, especially after she mentioned the door I had shattered. I would be caught as soon as my father saw; there was no way to avoid it. She was right—I had come too far to turn back now.

"Okay, I'll do it."

The woman squeezed her eyes shut.

"Are you sure you want me to?" I continued.

The woman hesitated, almost as if she couldn't believe I had agreed.

"Yes. I'm sure. I'm probably going to scream, though, so don't be scared."

"Oh boy," I said while closing my eyes. I felt sharpness in the pit of my stomach.

"Okay I'm ready."

"What if I'm not strong enough to chop all the way through?" I asked, hoping she'd change her mind and call it off.

"If we can't get through the bone then we'll loosen the strip around my arm. I'll bleed out. I'd rather that than stay down here forever."

I guess that made sense, as much as any of this made sense, anyway. This was truly a move of desperation on her part; she was ready to die if it didn't work. In a way, I admired her courage.

I took a deep breath and then lifted the hatchet. "Okay, on the count of three..."

"Don't count, just do it!"

I held the hatchet over my head, suddenly not sure if I could bring myself to go through with it. This had turned into so much more than I had bargained for. Then, in the midst of my hesitation, the woman screamed.

"Wait!"

I stopped.

"I just had another idea."

"Really?" I lowered the blade, a wave of relief washing over me.

"Maybe... I dunno maybe we can try a shim."

"What's a shim?"

"Like a flat piece of metal. See if you can find a flat piece of metal."

"How am I going to break the chain with that?"

"You're not. But you might be able to stick it in these cuffs so that we can unclick them. Kind of like unlocking a door with a credit card. It's a longshot but that's all I can think of."

"What's a credit card?"

"Don't worry about it. Just bring me a piece of metal. I'll show you," she said, and then I remembered all the empty beer cans littering the yard where my father had been shooting. If we could open up one those cans and unroll it, it just might work.

"Hang on, I think there's something up in the yard that we can use," I said, relieved that we were going to try something that didn't involve chopping off her hand.

I crawled out of the chamber, down the corridor and up the ladder. As I ascended into the shed, my vision, having become accustomed to the darkness, was hazy, but I felt a presence behind me. I had always marveled at how shadows seemed absurdly long in the sunset, and as my head surfaced from the darkness below, I saw a shadow that seemed to similarly stretch across the floor.

But it wasn't sunset—only winter—and when I turned, the tall silhouette of a man stood before me in the doorway.

"Daddy..."

He stepped forward.

As my vision cleared, I saw before me a man whose grizzled beard was peppered with threads of ice. He wore a thick greatcoat and the tip of his nose, in shadows beneath his hood, was black and swollen. Across his chest he held a long rifle, and the tips of his leather boots were stained in blood.

"I'm not your Daddy," said a husky, unfamiliar voice.

When the stranger pulled off his hood, the frozen snot under his nostrils and his frost laden eye lashes became exposed, and I wasn't sure who looked worse, the woman or the stranger.

"Who are you?"

"I'm looking for a man," he replied, staring right at my busted eye. He seemed like he was about to ask me about it, but I spoke first.

"How'd you find us?"

"I followed the tire tracks."

"Are you gonna hurt us?"

"No, I'm not going to hurt you."

"Then you came to help us?"

"You keep saying us. Who else is here?"

"There's a lady down there."

"There is?"

"Yeah I'm trying to get her out."

"Show me."

I descended into the tunnel and the stranger followed, hunching to fit through the corridor. I crawled into the chamber through the hole I had made earlier, but the stranger was too big to fit, so he ripped down the door entirely. As the wood shattered it sounded like ice cracking, and the stranger stood aghast upon sight of the prisoner.

"You have to help me! Please help me!" said the woman.

The stranger stood silent and still for a moment, and then glanced back down the corridor. He turned back to me with his mouth agape.

"What the hell?" he asked, almost as if asking himself.

"Please... *please* before he comes back...," she pled.

The tension on the stranger's face melted away as if he suddenly understood everything. He climbed over the bar lock and examined the woman's shackles.

"What's this?" he asked while lifting the strip of blanket I had tied around her arm.

"Please—just help me free. We don't have time. He could return any moment," she begged.

The stranger untied the strip and dropped it on the ground. "Give me that hatchet," he said, pointing to the tool on the floor behind me.

"Are you going to chop off her hand?"

"Am I going to *what?*"

"Chop off her hand," I said again while handing him the hatchet.

The stranger shook his head in disbelief. "No, I'm not going to chop off her hand. I'm going to break the chain."

The stranger rested his rifle against the wall and the woman assumed her position behind the pole, her shackles stretched against the black metal. "Stand back, boy," he said, so I slid behind him, my back against the cold stone. "And you—brace yourself," he said to the woman.

The stranger swung the hatchet down on the rusted chain.

"It's not working. You have to swing harder."

The stranger kicked the rotted door remnants to the side and then shifted his angle. "Okay ready," he said, before swinging the hatchet down once more.

Again the chain did not break.

"I'm going to need something heavier than this," said the stranger, shaking his head. "What else you got? Maybe an axe or something? I don't know if I can swing it down here but we can try."

I was about to answer that yes, we did have an axe, but before I could speak we were all distracted by the sound of tires in the snow.

"Oh my god… he's here," I said.

The stranger stalled for a moment and the woman began to weep. As we stood in silence, a truck door slammed shut up above.

"Who's here?"

"My Daddy," I whispered.

The stranger looked up. We listened to my father screaming at and beating on the truck.

"Is he the one who did all this?" asked the stranger, drawing his eyes back to me.

I didn't know what to say and the woman looked

away, trembling.

"He in a truck?" continued the stranger, having noticed her reaction.

I nodded.

The stranger looked down the corridor and then back into the chamber. He put down the hatchet and picked up his rifle. "Wait here," he said while cocking the weapon.

The woman and I waited in the chamber, shivering from both the cold and our fear as the stranger walked down the corridor. As he climbed the ladder, his feet quickly disappeared from our view. I turned off the flashlight and huddled close to her in the darkness. She pulled the striped blanket over us and said she wished her hands were unshackled—not so she could be free, but so she could hold me close to her.

After a silence that seemed to last forever, we heard the shouting of men. It evolved in a chaotic crescendo, climaxing with a single gunshot that thundered from above. We remained in the depths below, waiting for a man to return to the chamber, dreading which man it might be.

epilogue:
The Earth Itself Breaking

35
September 7, 1936

All paths are consumed in a choking cold blackness.

With no food for days, her warden and caretaker seemingly gone forever, she fears she too must soon depart.

As temperatures tumble, she seeks warmth and again finds herself barred from salvation. She curls into the fetal position in a struggle to survive the night.

Drifting into a slumber that merges with death, she opens her eyes upon hearing the gateway creak open. A pale shadow stands in the egress. She struggles to her feet and lets the stranger silently lead her away.

36
The Land of Nod

The weather had eased up over the past few days, and the snow seemed a little less powdery. The temperature hadn't risen quite enough for the leafless branches to start dripping, but that time appeared to be soon coming.

Wolves could, in normal times, go weeks without food, and the pack had eaten only days ago when they plundered the cabin in the woods. But that had been the first time in ages, it seemed, that they had eaten. The woodlands had remained barren, with nary a promising scent or footprint found, and the wolves' bellies rumbled and beckoned. C'naal could count the ribs of every wolf, several ready to collapse at any moment. In desperation he led the others back to the cabin, hoping that it would again prove to be a productive food source.

Although the constant humming no longer guided their passage, they remembered how to find the cabin. They entered the structure and found the interior bespattered by their earlier markings. The scent of deer, while faded, also remained on the cold wood floor, and when C'naal licked the surface he could still taste the coppery blood. The metal box that had once been their salvation was again upright, but this time when the wolves knocked it over, it was empty.

C'naal went out to the porch and peered into the foggy forest, unsure what to do next. The lifeless trees, their canopies shrouded in the whiteness, seemed like towering, crooked bars in the mist. As he gazed upon the wasteland, he suddenly heard distant sounds of unrecognized creatures—sounds that seemed to have their own rhythms.

Two tall shadows emerged from the fog. Although their two-legged gait seemed awkward, C'naal marveled at their upright locomotion, for these figures were unlike anything he had heretofore witnessed. He had, however, heard legends of such dangerous beasts—these creatures that were called men.

As the figures approached, C'naal realized two were in fact three—two afoot and one carried. The largest, which C'naal dubbed The Cold One, had a countenance of authority as he carried the smallest, which C'naal called The Child. The third figure, which appeared to be a female, was sickly and frail, and had to lean on the man for every stride, so C'naal called her The Punished.

The pack joined the clever wolf outside after hearing him softly growl. He signaled for them to spread out to more easily surround their prey. The wolves hurried into the mist, some ducking behind trees to the left and others to the right. The rest hustled forth diagonally in order to trap them from behind. C'naal waited on the porch to serve as a distraction while the pack assumed their positions.

When the figures advanced, C'naal saw upon their flesh an artificial fur and knew at once they were denizens of a faraway land. The Cold One, whom the woman seemed to follow, made sounds far deeper than the others, although he said little and seemed to speak only in response to the high pitched vocalizations of The Child. The Punished, perhaps too damaged to speak, made no sounds at all.

When the wind changed directions, C'naal recognized The Cold One's scent, and knew the structure upon which he was perched belonged to him. The Cold One locked eyes with the black wolf and halted before signaling the woman to also pause. He gently placed The Child on the snow and brought forth from behind him a black metal staff with a wooden handle. The Child hid behind the man, who raised the metal staff, pointing it at C'naal. C'naal stepped down from the porch and walked calmly towards him, not once breaking his gaze.

"Stay back!" shouted The Cold One as he made a clicking sound with the black metal.

When C'naal paused, about a dozen yards from his prey, the other wolves emerged from the mist and surrounded the three companions. The Cold One began to frantically rotate, pointing the metal staff at one wolf, then another, each motion more erratic than the last as the circle of wolves contracted. About halfway around he stopped and spun back towards C'naal.

"I said stay the fuck back!" he again screamed, while taking a step towards C'naal. The Punished began to tremble and The Child gripped the man's leg, his arms flopping to the ground as the man thrust forward.

The wolves assessed the group to determine which of the three would be the easiest target. They eliminated The Cold One forthwith for he was by far the most powerful, especially compared to the others who were either sickly or small, or both. Of those remaining, The Punished would provide more sustenance, for she was far larger than The Child. She was also unlikely to escape since every pace seemed a struggle on her withered legs. Meanwhile, The Child seemed to also be in poor health, for the scent of affliction wept from a gaping lesion below his eye. The combination of his condition and small stature would normally make him the target, but for some reason he seemed to be closely guarded by the man. C'naal couldn't understand why The Cold One would keep such feeble companions, who served only to weaken his advance.

After their silent deliberation, it was clear no one could decide which of the weak to target—it would have to be a decision made instinctively by whichever pack member first rushed in.

As the circle of wolves tightened, mere yards from their victims, The Cold One raised the metal staff towards the sky. It unleashed a crack like the earth itself breaking; like some perverse thunder roaring through nature.

The wolves all cringed and retreated. Some yelped

and cowered behind trees.

As he lowered the staff, a light smoke trickled upwards from it. C'naal knew at once the source of The Cold One's strength—it was a power with which the pack could not contend.

The Cold One rotated his body again, pointing the metal at several of the wolves as they withdrew. Then again he pointed it at C'naal, who remained far closer than the others, staring him down.

"Get in the truck," said The Cold One to his companions as he motioned towards a large machine, almost half the width of the cabin, standing on four round black feet.

The Punished and The Child entered the machine, followed by The Cold One, who pointed his staff all the while at C'naal. Once the three companions were inside, The Cold One enclosed them within the structure, and the wolves began approaching it in a circular formation once more.

The machine began to growl while spewing a toxic black smog from its rear. The smoke reeked of a virulence far more noxious than anything the wolves had ever beheld, so vile in fact that those in its wake began to gag and retreat. The machine then began to roll forward, several of the wolves scampering from its path as it fearlessly advanced. Carrying off their would-be prey, the machine quickly disappeared into the white desolation, leaving two long, continuous trails in the snow as evidence of its departure.

C'naal and the wolves looked at one another, not

Benjamin

quite understanding what had happened or how close they had come to destruction. With their heads down and nowhere left to turn, the wolves followed the path of the machine into the unknown, unsure when, if ever, they might feed again.

Acknowledgements

There are numerous individuals who provided input and feedback in various ways during the writing of this book. Those who stand out are Harriette Sackler, for multiple reviews and commentary on many different levels; Jessie Culotta, for reminding me how to write proper English; Jannalex Alviarez, for her great eye for artwork and formatting; and last but not least my mother, Fortuna Scheige, for reading more versions of this book than perhaps even I did and providing valuable criticism throughout. Others who provided helpful input during the process of writing and editing this book are Erika Villoldo, my sister Susan-Lisa Gvinter, and my father Steven Scheige. It really is amazing how many obvious errors and features I, as the author, failed to see and without the contributions of the friends and family listed above this book would have come out differently.

I would be remiss by failing to acknowledge my influences for this book, among which are Gene Wolfe, for proving that prose can sound like poetry; Dan Simmons, for his ability to combine disparate ideas and forms into a single, meaningful whole; David Lynch, for his masterful uses of metaphor and allegory; Atom Egoyan, for his technique of late revelation; and Stanley Kubrick, for his attention to detail.

About the Author

Rob is an insurance/space industry professional, horror lover and former party kid. His father used to read him Tales from the Crypt as bedtime stories, which explains a thing or two. He loves all forms of art, playing chess, dancing in front of the mirror and is an avid reader of fiction and non-fiction alike.

He lives in the Washington, DC area and can be reached at: bringbackbenjamin@gmail.com

A Note on Sources

While this novella is a work of fiction, the section titled "Bounties" is sadly true. There is a plethora of information about thylacines available, both in written form and on the internet. Some of the sources that were used in Benjamin, and that I would recommend to anyone interested in learning more, include:

- The Thylacine Museum (www.naturalworlds.org). This is probably the best online resource with many great pictures.

- www.messybeast.com/extinct/thylacine

- *Thylacine: The Tragic Tale of the Tasmanian Tiger.* By David Owen.

- *The Last Tasmanian Tiger: The History and Extinction of the Thylacine.* By Robert Paddle.

- www.wikipedia.org

- I should also mention *The Hunter*, a fictional movie (also based on a book) starring Willem DaFoe that was the impetus for my interest in thylacines.

- Videos of Benjamin, such as those described in this book, can be found on YouTube.

- Although it wasn't used as a resource for this book, for more general information about the ongoing mass extinction, I'd recommend *The Sixth Extinction* by Elizabeth Kolbert.

The lamentable tale of the thylacine is unfortunately far from unique. One needs to look no further than the great auk—a flightless, penguin-like bird that once numbered in the millions across the North Atlantic. It was hunted to extinction in the 1800s mostly by sailors looking for food and feathers, sometimes slaughtering them by the thousands in ghastly displays that included plucking the feathers off live birds and then flinging them into the sea to die. The last two great auks were found incubating an egg on an island near Reykjavik. They were strangled to death by two men who stomped on their egg during the course of the struggle. And so it was that the last great auk departed from our world before even taking its first breath.

There are countless species today facing the same

grim fate as the thylacine. In terms of megafauna, there are only 5 Northern white rhinos left in the world (all of which are in captivity). There are also only 40 Javan rhinos, 19 Amur leopards, and 3 Kashmir musk deer known to exist in the wild. Other species, such as lions, giraffes, and African elephants, while not yet critically endangered, have rapidly dwindling populations largely due to habitat destruction and poaching and may soon join the ranks of the extinct. These of course are only representatives from the more charismatic classes—even broader destruction is being wrought on smaller creatures—amphibians, insects, corals, and fish.

The California condor is the largest bird in North America, with a wingspan of up to 10 feet. It became critically endangered over the course of the 20th century due to habitat destruction and poaching. In 1987 the US government captured the last 22 remaining birds in the wild and began a captive breeding program. Four years later, they began reintroducing them into the wild. Today there are almost 500 California condors alive—half in the wild and half in captivity where breeding to save the species continues to this day.

By the time Benjamin was left to die alone in the cold, it was too late for her kind. But it isn't too late for the extant.

Made in the USA
Columbia, SC
20 November 2017